He wasn't just walking, he was swaggering

Lauren watched nervously as he approached. Granted, she'd made a terrible mistake trying to manipulate Richard. But, damn it, that didn't give him the right to start acting like a caveman....

She had no time for further thought. He wrapped an arm around her waist and pulled her close. At the soft collision of their bodies, her breath escaped on a little puff.

His mouth moved hungrily over hers, immediately scattering her indignation to the wind. She became heedless of anything save the scent and strength and sensuality of the man.

"Don't!" she uttered when he finally lifted his head. "Don't stop...."

Marion Smith Collins lives in her native Georgia with her husband, whom she met while studying journalism at the University of Georgia. They share a love of art, travel, oceans and beaches, and have two children.

This prolific author's seventh Harlequin Temptation, *For Love or Money*, combines warmth with the glamour and sophistication of old money and Thoroughbred horses.

Books by Marion Smith Collins

For Love or Money

MARION SMITH COLLINS

Harlequin Books

TORONTO • NEW YORK • LONDON
AMSTERDAM • PARIS • SYDNEY • HAMBURG
STOCKHOLM • ATHENS • TOKYO • MILAN

To Maureen Walters, my agent and my friend.

Published July 1986

ISBN 0-373-25214-5

Printed in Canada

1

"WOULD YOU MARRY ME, LAUREN?" The tall man who had been striding at her side stopped abruptly.

Lauren Wilding took another two steps forward, away from the warm hand at her back. *And they lived happily ever after*, she thought jubilantly. But that line was supposed to be delivered at the end of the story, not the beginning. A bead of perspiration trickled between her breasts, distracting her.

She turned to face him. "You do pick your times, Gannon." Her words were accompanied by a lazy smile.

Richard Gannon's perceptive gaze took in their surroundings. When his eyes returned to hers, he met her smile with a wry grin and a shrug of his wide shoulders. "You're absolutely right. See the effect you have on me?" he teased. But there was a watchful, waiting air about him.

She could imagine this dynamic man wearing just such an expression while dominating the boardroom of any major corporation. Powerful and intelligent, Richard Gannon was a very special person in this world, and he had just asked her to marry him.

"Time seems to be a major problem where we're concerned," he went on. "Nevertheless, I do want an answer. Will you?"

Lauren didn't hesitate any longer. Her smile spread until she was sure it lit up the cavernous room. "Yes, Richard. I'd like to marry you," she said, trying hard to keep the note of triumph out of her voice. "I'd like that very much."

A brilliant spark flared in Richard's eyes, burned fiercely there for a moment and finally subsided to leave them a smoldering, smoky gray. He loved this woman with an intensity that, six months ago, he wouldn't have believed possible. In fact, six months ago neither love nor marriage had been high on his list of priorities.

That was before he'd met Lauren, though, and now she was his. A thrill of possession threatened to blow the cover on his restraint.

Suddenly he narrowed his eyes. Deliberately suspending his feeling of elation for a moment, he searched her features. Despite Lauren's acceptance of his marriage proposal he realized he was getting mixed signals. She seemed happy, but he could see no deep, overwhelming emotion in her expression. *Keep it loose, keep it light*, he told himself. Considering his own feelings, that wasn't going to be easy.

Dismissing his vague misgivings and disregarding the scores of people who surged and ebbed around the two of them, he dropped the suitcase he'd been carrying and reached for her. His large hands framing her face, his fingers tangling her hair, he murmured softly, "My darling, do you know how very much I love you? You've made me the happiest man in the world." A trace of amusement passed across his features, diluting the seriousness there. "That phrase may be trite, but it's true."

Lauren's answer came after the blink of an eye. "I love you, too, Richard." Indifferent to the split stream of humanity passing them, she reached up to slide her fingers between the collar of his crisp white shirt and his tailored gray suit, pulling his head down toward her face.

Richard's kiss was one of the nicest things about him, she mused as his mouth covered hers. Sweetly moist and flatteringly hungry, his lips were firm and exciting, and very, very knowing. She closed her eyes, experiencing the same disorientation she always felt when he did this to her. She would have to work on that, she thought dazedly; she couldn't lose her bearings every time he took her in his arms.

But the scent of him undermined all her resolve. His subdued after-shave seemingly overpowered the myriad scents of the Thirtieth Street train station. And the sound of his accelerated breathing drowned out voices, footsteps, travel announcements and echoes.

Then, without releasing her lips, he changed the angle of the kiss. Slipping one hand down to the small of her back, he held her closer, against the growing sign of his arousal, and all at once her senses scattered. Responding out of control to the man who held her, Lauren struggled to master the passion that seemed to turn her bones to liquid. But the kiss was too powerful, too sensual.

"Hey, buddy! There's a hotel down the street!" A muffled wolf whistle followed the words.

Richard broke off the kiss, raised his head and grinned rather hazily at the burly man in workman's clothes who had interrupted them.

"Go to it, friend." The man chuckled and shook his head before moving on.

Feeling Lauren attempt to straighten in his arms, he loosened his hold, but didn't release her. Lord, she was potent, and he was in a distinctly embarrassing situation. "Are you all right?" he asked.

"I'm not quite sure," she answered huskily. Her hand slid down to rest over his thundering heart. "Give me a minute."

He smoothed back the silky strands of pale gold hair that he had disarranged, surprised to see that his hand was shaking slightly, and he smiled down into her eyes. He loved her eyes. One of the first things he'd noticed about her were those wide, clear eyes the color of mountain blueberries—a fathomless indigo with a touch of purple in their depths. The lashes that surrounded them were thick and spiky, giving her face a deceptively innocent look.

He had been deceived when he'd first met her, thinking her much younger than her thirty-one years. In fact, he'd wondered at the attention she'd paid to him, a thirty-eight-year-old man, when there were plenty of younger bachelors at the party. With women he'd learned to be...cautious. But, then, she had told him her name. A Wilding, particularly a Wilding who had distinguished herself in the business world of Philadelphia, certainly wasn't going to be tempted by his money or his success.

"Do you really have to go to Saratoga Springs?" he asked, wishing he hadn't committed himself to so many projects this year. If nothing went wrong, though, he would have some free time after this trip.

Lauren touched his face, tracing the masculine line of his jaw with an affectionate finger. Richard was an exceptionally good-looking man, rugged rather than refined. There was an inherent strength and sureness in him that had appealed to her from the first. She smiled regretfully. "My parents are expecting me."

"And you're going to be there for a month." It wasn't a question. He knew that the Wilding family gathered twice a year in Saratoga Springs. Once for the racing season, which lasted the entire month of August, and then for two weeks at Christmas.

"I need the vacation, Richard. It's the first time in eight years I've been able to take the whole month. Besides, it's a little late for a change of plans now. Your plane leaves in less than four hours."

Giving a hefty sigh, Richard kissed her forehead. "And I have to finish at the office and check on one of my kids before I leave."

Richard was active in a Big Brother type of organization, and Lauren knew how much the kids meant to him. "Trouble?" she asked, a worried frown on her face.

"Probably not." He folded her close again and gently stroked her back. "I'm going to miss you like hell, you know," he murmured.

Not only would he miss her companionship, he added to himself, but he would miss the sight of her. She was so perfectly put together, almost intimidatingly so. Her hair was chin length, slightly longer in front than in the back, like shining parentheses framing her face; whispy bangs were swept away from the side part. When she moved her head with the self-confident little toss that was becoming so familiar to him, the fine strands moved, too, only to settle immediately back where they belonged, as though they knew their place. She wore a sunny sleeveless linen shift that also seemed to defy not only the July heat but the ferocity of the embrace they'd just shared. Her image was cool and collected, as always.

Picking up her suitcase again, he draped an arm over her shoulder, his reluctant footsteps guiding them down the steps toward the train tracks. Her long legs adjusted her stride to his, easily, effortlessly. That was another of the many things he loved about her. Their fit was perfect. A tall man, he appreciated her height of five-foot-eight. He could imagine walking with her this way in many settings throughout their lives. Years from now, when they stood less erect, when the passion was less intense—if such a day ever came—they would still be a good fit.

Unable to resist, he put his lips against her temple. "I should be home from Amsterdam by Friday night. I'll call you."

"That reminds me—" Lauren stopped walking to rummage in the large purse that rested against her hip. "I'd better give you a number. The phone in the main part of the house is in Daddy's name, but there's a separate line into the wing where I stay. It's unlisted." She found a pen and note pad and copied the number down for him.

When he glanced at the paper and stuffed it into his pocket, she smiled to herself. He wouldn't have to look at it again, she knew; Richard had a memory that astounded her. "Shall I expect you on Saturday, then?"

"I'll be there, but it may be late. I have to go into the office first thing in the morning."

"Are you sure you want to go to the Courtlands' party Saturday night, then? I know it's the kickoff for the August festivities, but we could certainly skip it if you'd rather."

"We may as well get the inquisition over with," he told her with mock trepidation. "All your friends and relatives will want their chance to pass judgment on me."

She laughed. "There won't be any of that, Gannon. I'm known for making wise decisions."

"When do you want to tell your family about us?"

"I think I'll wait until you get there," Lauren hedged.

She had described her family to him in great detail when she had first invited him to join them in Saratoga Springs. He already knew the Wildings were a large, diverse group, but a loving family nonetheless. Each member was definitely a part of the whole. Her father, William "Red" Wilding, had come off a New England farm with a genius for mechanical engineering. He'd made a fortune in manufacturing, and married Sarah Slade, the debutante daughter of a federal judge.

Marshall was the eldest of the Wildings' four children; Lauren considered him a bit of a stuffed shirt. As managing director of their father's many businesses here in Philadelphia he was burdened with the kind of responsibilities Richard easily understood. Slade, the second brother, bred and raced horses in Kentucky and was the closest both in age and outlook to Lauren. Only Lynn, Lauren's sister, wouldn't be traveling to Saratoga this year, because she was eight months pregnant and wasn't up to the trip from her home in California.

Despite Lauren's disclaimer, he also knew that her choice of a husband would be avidly dissected and discussed. Interest wouldn't be confined to her immediate family, numerous aunts, uncles and cousins, either. He would also be the subject of speculation by the entire strata of society who spent the month of August in Saratoga Springs, New York, for the racing season.

Richard suspected, without conceit, that he would not be found wanting. "Coward," he accused gently.

"Coward, am I?" She placed her palm against his chest and pushed. "I'm not being cowardly." She sighed. "Well, maybe a little bit. My parents will be so excited their old-maid daughter is finally going to take the plunge that I'll be deluged with nosy questions."

"And that, my lazy love, would drive you to distraction."

Lauren laughed at the qualified endearment. Richard knew very well that her energy level on the job was legendary. But it was a joke between them and a truth she readily admitted; she would work like a demon to finish a task so that she could be luxuriously lazy afterward. Outside her office she hated schedules and digital clocks, considering them too precise for the precious few leisure hours she managed to scrape together. She loved books, music and sunbathing, all delightful pursuits that could be enjoyed on a whim, without expending physical energy.

Blue eyes sparkling, she tilted her head to the side and smiled mischievously. "Gannon," she chided gently. "What an observation to make about the woman you've just asked to marry you. Simply because I don't like to sweat . . ."

Grinning, he conceded, "And I do."

"I don't mind if you want to ruin your knees with all that running and tennis and stuff. Just don't expect me to join you. When I'm not getting my mental exercise in the boardroom I'd rather float around on a raft in a heated pool."

"You wouldn't have gotten where you are if you were as lazy as you pretend to be," he accused lightly.

Where Lauren *was* was at the head of a thriving chain of baby boutiques that stretched from San Francisco to New York. Though the initial financing had come from her father, she had repaid every penny with interest over the past eight years. And for the past two of those, Tender Age had become more of a success than even she had dreamed.

"Well, I intend to be as slow-moving as a turtle for a few days, anyway." A work-packed week had just passed while she had been trying to prepare for her first lengthy vacation in eight years. It seemed as though she'd barely had eight hours sleep in the past seventy-two, and she planned to make up for the loss over the next few days.

Just the thought of being in her parents' home, where she wouldn't have to lift a finger if she didn't choose to, caused her footsteps to slow to an amble. She could rest more easily, too, now that all her careful planning had paid off with a proposal from Richard. A delicious kind of weariness settled over her.

He matched his gait to hers. "So we go to the party at the risk of your sanity?"

She had to prod her tired brain back to the original subject of the conversation—her being driven to distraction by curious well-wishers. She shuddered in distaste at the thought of facing that alone. "I suppose so. Everyone will have heard of you by reputation, you know. But really, they'll probably be thrilled. You are exactly right for me; they'll see that." She shifted her head against his shoulder so she could look up at him, a complacent smile curving her lips.

"Just as long as you know it," he growled against her ear.

The train coughed and the conductor called, "Board!" as they neared the platform. Suddenly Richard turned her in his arms, creating a warm haven for her. "I hate leaving you," he grated. His mouth was tender and loving as it sought hers in a poignant goodbye kiss.

"Board!" Once again the conductor's voice intruded.

Gripping her shoulders, Richard studied her for a long minute, then smiled enthusiastically. "Come with me." It was not a request; it was a command.

Lauren was not used to being given commands. "What?" she asked blankly.

"Come with me to Amsterdam. There's no reason not to, and after all—" he smiled "—we are engaged."

"Don't be silly," she responded too quickly. If she had stopped to think, she would have known it was the wrong thing to say. On occasion she had to remind herself not to underestimate Richard's strength of purpose and his uncanny ability to read her mind.

"Did I miss something here?" he asked in a strange tone.

Lauren felt her heart descend to her toes. Richard's brow furrowed with his quiet question. His jaw firmed to an angle that she was unfamiliar with—and didn't like at all. His entire countenance had darkened and he had dropped his hands from her shoulders. He took only one step back, but his retreat was farther, much farther than that.

"I don't want to walk away from you, Lauren, not right now," he said decisively. "We can get you on my flight tonight, or I'll wait and go tomorrow. One day won't matter."

A frown marred the smooth arch of her brows. He spoke as if it were a foregone conclusion that she would just drop everything and fall in with his plans. "I can't," she protested.

"Why not? You're on vacation."

"Richard, you'll be working while you're there. You won't have time for a tagalong." He looked as if he were about to argue, but she didn't pause. "Besides, Mother and Daddy are expecting me. There's a lot to do before the season starts next weekend and they're counting on me to do quite bit of it," she reasoned soothingly.

"You?" A quirk of a smile teased his lips.

"Me." She kissed the stubborn thrust of his chin. "You do understand, don't you, that I can't leave?"

"I believe I'm being manipulated," he accused lightly, but his attempt at humor was strained.

Lauren conceded silently that he was right, but manipulating a man with such a forceful personality was not as easy as he made it sound.

"Hell, no, I don't understand," he continued. "It's only for four days. You say you love me . . ."

"I do love you!" Lauren searched her mind for another excuse and came up blank. She didn't want to face this particular discussion right now. Her well-thought-out plans had come to fruition more quickly than she'd expected. He'd proposed marriage, just as she had intended for him to do, but he wasn't supposed to be making demands on her, she thought, suddenly irritated.

Determinedly tamping down her irritation, she touched his mouth with a well-manicured finger to stop the accusation she knew was on the tip of his tongue. "I do," she repeated more softly. "Richard, listen. We haven't had a chance to discuss plans, but I was hoping, that is . . ."

"Hoping what?" he asked. He folded his arms over his broad chest. His amusement had totally vanished again and he wore a faintly detached expression that said "convince me."

Honestly! She took a breath and plunged in. "I'll be in Saratoga for a whole month with my family, and I thought it would—might be—a good time to plan a wedding."

It was obvious that was the last thing he expected her to say. "A wedding?" he said slowly, dropping his arms.

Lauren nodded, smiling with a becoming shyness—she hoped.

"How will you be able to do that if you aren't going to tell them until I get there?"

Damn. She hadn't thought of that. "Well, of course I'll have to tell my mother and father," she said, pretending to be shocked that he wouldn't understand a daughter's concerns. "It will take some rush planning, but we could get married at the end of the month. That is if you want to, if you don't have any commitments."

The inner voice Richard depended on to warn him when something wasn't quite right was suddenly quiet. All the reservations that had been niggling at him were swept away in a surge of joy at her words. Without warning, he wrapped her in an enthusiastic bear hug and lifted her off her feet. He swung her around once, then let her toes touch the pavement. "If I want to! No commitment would stand in the way of our wedding, don't you know that? Ah, Lauren, I love you." He brought her into a closer embrace, scattering tender kisses over her face, ending at her lips.

They had known each other for six months, but the total days they'd spent together were less than twenty. Maybe it was natural for her to still have a certain reserve toward him, he decided. Hell, they hadn't even made love yet. Ah, well, all that would change, now that he had a promise from her. They would spend hours together. As soon as he got back from Amsterdam he would have time to work on making their relationship what it should be.

"Board!" The train began to make warning sounds, like a large animal straining at its leash.

"I've got to go," Lauren murmured, though she discovered to her own surprise that she would have liked to stay within the secure circle of his arms for a while longer.

"I know." He sighed and released her. "I'll miss you, Wilding," he said, tweaking her nose. He hefted her case up to a waiting, widely grinning porter.

"I'll miss you, too, Gannon." Lauren suddenly realized that she meant the words. The temperature of the late-July afternoon seemed to drop to a wintry chill at the thought of their parting.

Holding one elbow securely, he guided her chivalrously to the platform. She climbed aboard the train. His fingers were reluctant as they trailed from her bare arm, as though unwilling to break even the small contact. "You get started right away on those wedding plans," he ordered, his voice low and husky. "And rest up before next weekend. I plan to tire you all over again." She was surprised that her voice was as husky as his. "Okay, Gannon. Bye."

He gave her a sexy half grin. "Goodbye, love."

Still bemused by his grin and the accompanying glint in his eye, Lauren walked right by her compartment and had to backtrack, searching along the aisle until she found the number. The effect Gannon had on her wasn't altogether reassuring; in fact, it worried her. What had become of her objective nature?

She dropped her heavy purse on the seat and sat herself down with a sigh. Almost warily her eyes sought the tall figure of her fiancé through the dusty window.

Gannon's hands were thrust deep into his pockets and he rocked slightly on his heels in the manner of a man congratulating himself. The smile that curved his talented mouth as he met her gaze was vastly satisfied.

Forgetting her concern, Lauren chuckled to herself and blew him a kiss as the train began to move. When he was out of sight her eyes focused on her own hazy reflection in the glass and she saw—as she knew she would—the same satisfied expression there. Chewing her lower lip, she allowed herself one further moment of uncertainty, wondering if she had done the right thing.

Then she linked her fingers together under her chin, squeezing them in delight. Right or not, the deed was done. Maybe not as gracefully as it could have been, but done. She was getting married!

Lauren had begun thinking about marriage almost a year ago. Here she was, the owner of a string of baby shops, and the chances of her ever having a baby of her own were growing slimmer every year. Though times had changed and she could probably have managed a child and a career without the benefit of marriage, she discovered that she was more conservative than she'd thought. She wanted a baby, but first she wanted a husband, so she had started looking.

She had decided the man must be healthy, intelligent and of good character—three qualities she wanted to pass on to her offspring. And his life-style must be compatible with hers. That is, he must be busy and involved in his own career. She wanted a husband not a companion. He didn't have to be especially handsome, but she wanted him to be impressive-looking.

There had been only one further criterion, the most important one of all. He must be rich. Lauren was almost paranoid about some man marrying her for her money. She had come close to that tragedy when she was twenty-two, and the experience had left its scars. Since that time she'd been very careful of her feelings.

But how to be sure that her money didn't add one whit to her appeal? Simple. By marrying someone who was as wealthy or wealthier than she.

Relaxing against the padded seat, she let go a long sigh of relief and released her thoughts to the night she had met Richard Gannon.

Almost from the moment they'd been introduced she'd known that Richard fulfilled all her requirements, including the last one. He was a renowned financial wizard, founder and president of a firm that did consulting work for companies and countries all over the world. While it would be difficult to compete monetarily with the far-flung Wilding empire, he managed to do so wholly on his own.

She'd heard of him even before they met, since over the past few years he'd been praised by *Time*, applauded by *Newsweek*, not to mention being named Bachelor of the Year by *Cosmopolitan*.

Occasionally Lauren felt a pang of conscience for deciding cold-bloodedly to marry for money. But had Richard been King Midas himself she wouldn't have married him if she hadn't liked him . . . a lot. And she had no reservations about spending the rest of her life with him. Now he had proposed, she had accepted, and all that remained to be done was to plan the wedding.

However, when she replayed the conversation they'd just had, she dropped her hands into her lap and frowned, feeling the sense of misgiving return twofold. Richard had never made any demands on her before. She knew how strong he was; that was why she'd had to be so very careful in her campaign to make him fall in love with her. Despite all her meticulous research into his habits, into the legend that was Richard Gannon, occasionally she caught a glimpse of something beneath his polished facade that didn't fit what she knew of him, something that was not quite gentlemanly.

AN HOUR AFTER he put Lauren on the train, Richard sat in his office, looking beyond the window to the overcast skies that matched his mood. He missed her already.

He smiled, remembering that night half a year ago when they'd met. He'd watched her from the moment she'd arrived at the party. And she had watched him watching her. Carefully, almost skeptically, as though they'd each had to decide whether to chance a meeting, they'd circled the room.

It was by far the most intriguing encounter he'd ever had. She hadn't made a secret that she was attracted to him, but neither had she been blatant about it, as so many of the women he met would have been. They had figuratively danced around each other for the first hour or so, indulging only in the social chitchat that such functions call for.

Without saying a word, and in her own well-bred, ladylike way, she had indicated very clearly that she was interested.

Interested was too mild a word for what *he'd* felt. He was fascinated, bowled over by the self-confidence of the sleek blond beauty, that self-confidence—garnished with the slightest hint of arrogance—didn't diminish her attractiveness one iota as far as he was concerned. He'd never cared for clinging vines.

Together they had left the party early, and wandered the streets of Philadelphia for hours, stopping once for eggs and bacon at an all night café. They had talked nonstop and touched and kissed. For him, each touch, every kiss, had fueled fires ignited at the first glimpse of the beautiful woman in the midnight-blue dress that matched her eyes so perfectly.

The next day Gannon left for three weeks in Japan. He'd called her every night. His phone bill had been presented to him when he checked out of his hotel, with a red question mark penciled in by some curious clerk. He'd laughed.

His secretary interrupted his thoughts, bustling into the office, a pencil stuck haphazardly into the frizzled bun on top of her head, her arms loaded down with papers to be signed. "These are the last of them, Richard."

"Good." Gannon slashed his signature across several sheets before he lifted his head. "You know, Roxy, I'm looking forward to four whole days without your running around pushing papers in my face."

Their eyes met in amusement. Roxanne was well aware that the mundane office chores bored Richard to death. He'd much rather be working out a financial puzzle than attending to administrative duties.

"Four whole days without having to listen to you complain about it," she retorted.

He grinned. "Please have my luggage sent to the airport, Roxy. I have an errand to take care of before I leave. I'll grab a cab when I'm through. While I'm gone you can take some time off if you like."

Roxanne hid her surprise. Her employer paid extremely well, but he demanded near perfection for his money. "In case you didn't miss me, I just returned from vacation."

He shrugged. "Take some more. I'm feeling generous."

"In that case, maybe I should ask for a raise."

"You harpy, I already pay you more than you're worth," he answered in the same tone she had used. In reality Roxanne was priceless to him, and she knew it. He sobered. "Do you need more money, Roxy? You know you can have it."

"Of course not. I'd tell you if I did. What's brought all this on, Richard? You seem exceptionally softhearted today."

He waited a minute before answering. "You can congratulate me, Roxy," he said softly.

Roxanne had sent the roses, and put through the telephone calls to Lauren Wilding. She had noticed the softening in her boss's attitude, his tendency to drop his voice to an intimate purr when he talked to Lauren.

The signs were unmistakable to the secretary who, for ten years, had monitored his reaction to the women who had gone in and out of his life. It didn't take Sherlock Holmes to see that Richard Gannon was in love for the first time since she'd come to work for him. Though he had always seemed to have a full productive life, Roxanne had known that there was something missing, and he had finally begun to realize it. Her face relaxed into a smile.

"I'm very happy for you, Richard. If you weren't so picky it would have happened long ago." She was several years his senior, but his magnetic appeal wasn't lost even on her, and she had been happily married for twenty years.

"Ah, but this one was worth waiting for."

"When's the big day?"

"The end of the month. At her family's place in up-state New York, outside of Saratoga Springs." He tilted his chair back and linked his fingers behind his head, his mouth relaxing in a smile. "I've never been so happy, Roxy. Never really expected to be."

She was touched by his emotion. "Will I get an invitation?"

Feet flat on the floor, he leaned forward. "Are you kidding? You're my best friend, so I guess you're going to have to be my best man."

Roxy blushed, obviously flattered by the compliment. "Nonsense. A woman can't be a best man," she blustered. "You'll have to come up with a better one than that. Have you given her a ring yet?"

"A ring? Good Lord, I'd forgotten about a ring!" What must Lauren have thought? "I want it to be something very special." Frowning, he thought for a minute. A sapphire, the color of her eyes, maybe, or a yellow diamond that would reflect the sunshine in her smile, he thought, grinning whimsically. Whimsy certainly wasn't one of his usual traits, but he found himself enjoying the light-hearted feeling.

"Well, you're leaving in a couple of hours for the diamond capital of the world," observed Roxanne. "You ought to be able to find something."

"Right!" Gannon checked his watch. With a sudden burst of energy he swung back to the papers on his desk. "If I don't miss the plane."

GANNON STOOD at an apartment door on the second floor of a seedy, rundown building in the middle of a neighborhood surrounded on all sides by decay and hopelessness. His stomach was knotted in fury and frustration.

"When did he leave?" He asked the question of the indifferent woman who leaned against the jamb. His voice was quiet and dangerous, but she either didn't notice or didn't care that he was within inches of strangling her.

"I don't know," She waved wickedly long, red-tipped fingernails carelessly in the direction of the street. "He's always takin' off somewhere. I ain't seen him in close to a week, I guess. He's probably in the slammer."

Gannon tightened his fists to keep from shaking her until her teeth rattled. "Good God, woman! He's your son! Don't you care?"

The woman looked him straight in the eye. "Hell, no," she said without any emotion at all. "He ain't been nothin' but trouble for sixteen years. I'da been better off if he'd never been born."

Uttering a curse under his breath—a filthy, vulgar curse that would have shocked the people who knew him—Richard forced down his rage into a semblance of calm. "Will you call my secretary when you hear from him?"

Her expression, changing with the speed of lightning, became cunning and greedy. "I might. If it was made worth my while."

"You'll get paid when I see him," said Gannon, thoroughly sickened. "I'll be back Thursday night. If he comes here—" he couldn't bring himself to say *home* "—before that, tell him to call."

The woman shrugged and started to turn away, but suddenly his temper got away from him. He caught her arm in a grip of iron and spun her against the wall. His eyes blazed as he deliberately tightened his fingers. His words gritted out from between clenched teeth. "Do you hear me, you witch? I want to know where that boy is."

"Yeah, I hear you, Mr. Big Man," she muttered grudgingly.

Gannon released his grip. "Don't forget," he spat. He almost ran down the stairs and out onto the comparatively fresh air of the street. He took deep, restorative gulps, trying to calm his queasy stomach, and set off down the street, his long legs eating up the distance toward the closest intersection.

Violence in any form was abhorrent to him, but in the few minutes he'd faced that woman he'd wanted to kill her. His hands felt dirty; breathing hard, he pulled a clean handkerchief out of his pocket and wiped his palms.

Without conscious awareness of what he was doing, Richard sought a thought, a picture of something clean and beautiful, as he had done so many times when he was a child. He needed to purge the foulness from his mouth, the stench of greed and cunning from his nostrils in order to preserve his sanity. His mind pictured Lauren. Deliberately he forced the vision of her away, as if even his thoughts in these circumstances, these surroundings might soil her clean, beautiful image. He walked faster.

He didn't allow himself to think of her again until he was out of the area. When he'd settled into the seat of the taxi and was on his way to the airport he breathed a sigh of relief and permitted her to seep back into his thoughts like a warm comforting balm that soothed his raw emotions. Beautiful, wonderful Lauren. His wife to be.

2

LAUREN SAT at the Queen Anne desk in her mother's morning room. Situated at the back of the rambling Victorian house, the room and its twin, her father's study, gave vistas of gently rolling hillsides framed by the majestic mountains of upstate New York. She was addressing invitations for her parents' annual cocktail party, to be held in two weeks, after the Saratoga Springs yearling sale. She checked another name off and set the creamy envelope on the growing stack, carefully avoiding the rather garish ceramic giraffe that sat in a place of honor on the desk.

"Most of these people are Slade's friends, aren't they, Mother? Where is the rest of the list?" she asked absently. When she didn't get an answer she looked up. The sight of her mother brought a smile to her lips.

Sarah Wilding, looking more like forty than sixty, was comfortably but elegantly sprawled in an overstuffed chair across the room, going over the lists that invariably multiplied like rabbits when a social occasion or a charity benefit had to be planned. She was clenching a pencil between her teeth and her glasses had dipped until they were in danger of falling off the end of her nose.

Riffling through the papers in her hands one last time, she removed the pencil to speak. "I don't have it here. Maybe it's in the drawer of the desk." Hearing a sound, she looked up. "Oh, good, there you are, Shaw. Do you remember where I put my guest list?"

The butler answered from the doorway. "No, madam, I'm sorry." Indeed he almost did look regretful, if such an emotion could be interpreted from his starched countenance.

Lauren hid a smile. In all her life she'd never seen Shaw set aside his dignified manner, except when he couldn't fulfill the wishes of his mistress. Everyone in this household was devoted to the task of soothing the bumps of life out of her mother's path. Sarah was as soft and sweet as her delicate blond, blue-eyed appearance suggested. Gentle as summertime in the countryside, she was adored not only by the servants but by her family and her many friends.

Those who considered Sarah a lovely social butterfly didn't take into consideration the astounding amounts of money she raised for the many causes in which she was involved. If Sarah Wilding had ever turned her talents toward the business world, her fortunes would have rivaled those of her maverick husband.

"Well, I expect we'll find the other list somewhere." Sarah shrugged. "I can't worry about it today. Did you need me?" she asked the butler.

"I came to inquire, madam, if you would like a light supper before the party tonight. A chilled soup, perhaps, or a salad tray?"

"That's a wonderful suggestion, Shaw. If the party runs true to form we won't have anything before nine. And you know how grouchy we all get when we're hungry."

Shaw nodded, then caught himself. "Supper for how many, madam?"

Lauren mentally counted along with her mother. Marshall, his wife and two sons were in from Philadelphia to spend the month at their summer home nearby, so they would probably come over as soon as they unpacked. Slade wouldn't arrive until next week, and Lynne wasn't coming at all this year.

"Just eight Shaw, unless Mr. Wilding brings one of his cronies home from the golf course. Maybe you'd better tell Mrs. Hansen to prepare a bit extra in case. And set everything out on the sideboard. We'll serve ourselves."

The man looked puzzled, but was much too punctilious to question the numbers.

Sarah paused for effect. "Miss Lauren's fiancé, Mr. Richard Gannon, will be joining us."

A smile cracked the polished demeanor as Shaw turned toward her with a stiff little bow. "Please permit me to offer my best wishes, Miss Lauren."

She could see the speculation that lit his eyes, but of course he was correct about it. Marshall and his wife would also be polite and correct. Poor Marshall.

It was a shame he hadn't married someone who was more down to earth, someone who would puncture his balloon of pomposity occasionally. "Thank you, Shaw," she said, and sighed slightly.

The butler turned to leave, but she called him back. "Shaw, I almost forgot," she said carelessly. "Could you please have someone pick up Mr. Gannon at the airport at five?"

"Lauren! You're not going to meet him yourself?" said Sarah, surprise widening the clear blue eyes, then suspicion narrowing them.

Damn! That was a major mistake. The last thing she wanted was for her mother to suspect this marriage was anything but a passionate conclusion to a romantic affair. She had been very careful to play the part of a woman deeply in love when she told her parents about Gannon. "Well, I was helping you with the invitations," she offered rather lamely.

As an excuse it wasn't much, but her mother seemed to accept it. "They don't have to be mailed until next week. Leave them for now." Sarah looked pointedly at Lauren's attire. "I know you'll want to change before you go to the airport."

Lauren gave the butler a weak smile of dismissal, and after he'd left she eyed her mother cautiously.

Rescuing her glasses from their perch on the tip of her nose, Sarah folded them carefully and slipped them into a case before she spoke. "I must say, Lauren, you're acting very strangely about this whole affair."

Her mother hadn't accepted the excuse at all, Lauren realized. "Strangely? I don't know what you're talking about."

"When Lynne married—"

Lauren's whoop of laughter cut off the rest of the sentence. "Mother," she chided. "You know I'm nothing like Lynne."

Sarah smiled. "No, you aren't are you?" She paused. "You're sure there's nothing wrong?"

Lauren tossed the pen she'd been using aside and combed her fingers through her hair, arching her back slightly. "Nothing's wrong, mother. It's just . . ." She dropped her hands heavily into her lap and her smile faded. "You know what happened the last time I was engaged."

Sarah's features softened. "I know, dear. And I know how horribly you were hurt. But this is different. Richard Gannon is different."

Thank goodness, thought Lauren. "Rich, you mean," she said aloud.

"Lauren, don't be crude."

She shrugged. "At least there won't be a repeat of the same gossip."

"You were very young," her mother said, as she always did when the subject was mentioned.

"And gullible. Everyone in Saratoga and Philadelphia knew that Monty was a gold digger long before I did. Especially all the people he owed money to." She couldn't control the bitterness that stained her voice at the memory of the heartbreak she'd endured. She preferred to keep her personal and business life separate and private, but Monty had loved splashing the most confidential details of their engagement, and their plans for Tender Age, all over the newspapers. She supposed he'd hoped to impress his creditors, one of whom had called from Palm Beach, dunning her for payment of a shocking bill for clothing. The crowning touch had come when she found out he hadn't been alone on the trip.

"Thank goodness you didn't marry him."

"Yes. Thank goodness," she agreed with a cheerful smile. "Well, that's ancient history now, and if I'm to meet Gannon I'll have to change clothes."

A few minutes later Lauren had peeled off her jeans and shirt and stepped into the tub to sink under the surface of the scented water. She hoped she had soothed her mothers misgivings. She'd been walking on eggshells from the moment she'd told her parents she was going to marry Richard Gannon. They had obviously expected reactions from her that she hadn't been able to give.

She made a face at her image in the mirrored wall. If they thought she was going to moon around and subside into dreamy trances the way Lynne had done, they were doomed to disappointment. Even if she had been madly, wildly in love, she wasn't the type to behave that way. Her parents should know her better than that.

Having been honed in the world of business for the past eight years, she'd found that being practical was the most important lesson to learn. And her marriage would be run on practical lines.

She soaped a long leg and thought about sex, and Gannon. He would expect to sleep with her this weekend. The idea was...was what? she mused. Not unpleasant. A little scary after such a long time. Sex wasn't one of her favorite things.

The week had passed quickly. She had almost slept around the clock after her arrival. When she awoke her energy was up to its normal level. The rest of the week had been devoted to her parents—an unrushed, leisurely visit that had delighted them all.

Gannon had called twice and she'd enjoyed talking to him, but she hadn't spared much attention to thoughts of him other than the calls. Out of sight, out of mind, and that was the way it should be. No distracting desire, no yearning to see him when he was away, no longing to distract her from her work. This marriage would be perfect.

The thought of the marriage sparked another uncomfortable sensation. She had avoided telling her mother that they were planning to marry at the end of August, just four weeks away. Sarah thought she had plenty of time to make plans—and lists. She had better correct that impression soon, Lauren told herself, before Gannon arrived. He was bound to mention the wedding right off.

Fifteen minutes later she skipped lightly down the stairs, dressed in sharp white pants and a safari shirt. Her father was just coming in the front door, his endearingly ugly face slightly pink from the effects of the sun.

Lauren greeted him with an enthusiastic hug. "Hi, Daddy. I'm off to the airport."

Red Wilding smiled fondly at his youngest child. "At last I get to meet the man of the hour."

She tried to put a yearning lilt into her voice. "Yes. At last. Shall I take the Deusenberg?"

Red gasped.

"How about the Jeep, then?" She laughed. Her father was very protective of his aging vehicles. What horses were to Slade, old automobiles were to Red. Lauren was one of the few people he allowed to drive even the old Jeep, but she always asked permission first.

"You know the Jeep's yours for as long as you're here. Just don't put any scratches on it."

Lauren laughed again. "As though they'd be noticed among the dents and rust spots. Want to ride along?"

"I can withhold my curiosity for another hour. I probably need a shower."

She leaned back in his embrace and wrinkled her nose at him. "Well," she drawled, "now that you mention it . . ."

He slapped her bottom. "Brat! What time does his plane arrive?"

Lauren glanced automatically at the slim gold watch on her wrist. It said twelve-thirty. She'd forgotten to wind it again. She shrugged. "At five. What time is it now?"

"I'm going to buy you one of those watches with a battery," her father threatened affectionately. "A digital one."

"You'd just be wasting your money, Dad," she said lightly. "You know I'd never wear it. I'd much rather know that it was about twenty minutes till six than five thirty-seven." She planted a kiss on his scratchy cheek. "You need a shave, too."

"Yes, ma'am. And you'd better get going or you'll be late. It's four-thirty."

"Right." Lauren gave him a little salute.

He released her and watched as she headed for the door. "Lauren," he said softly. When she turned back to him he added, "He has a reputation for being a fine man. You know me—I'll have to see for myself, but I'm very happy for you."

Lauren swallowed a lump in her throat. She adored this rather blustery man who didn't often speak so seriously to her and seldom called her Lauren. "Thanks, Daddy," she said, even more softly.

"You seem less cold, more...mellow. I'll admit I've been worried about you."

Cold? "Worried?" She didn't understand.

He nodded and grinned ruefully. "You're too much like me, I'm afraid. You're amiable on the surface, but it isn't easy for you to really open up to people outside your family. An engagement to a thoroughly selfish young man didn't help, either."

Lauren slid her hands into her pockets and smiled. It was true; she was a lot like her father. "No, it didn't help," she agreed quietly.

"I hope this time you're ready to give your whole heart to this man, Lauren. A marriage isn't much without love."

"Of course I love him," she affirmed. *My kind of love is simply more comfortable,* she added silently.

"Then that's all that matters. You'd better scoot along to the airport."

LAUREN THOUGHT ABOUT her father's words on the way to the airport. His comments, delivered in the form of a warning, disturbed her. She was sure he hadn't seen beyond her subterfuge, but she wouldn't have wanted to cause either him or her mother to worry. *Cold.* The word came back to trouble her. She had avoided emotional involvement, that was all. Did that make her cold?

She wheeled the Jeep into the crowded parking lot of the private field adjacent to the airport. "Oh, dear," she muttered under her breath. The sleek silver Lear, its fusilage decorated with the red and black logo of Gannon Consultants, was parked at the edge of the runway amid the other private planes that were disgorging their elite passengers.

She jerked at the emergency brake and jumped out. Her eyes found him immediately, lounging near the fuel pumps, his back to her. His broad shoulders towered over the two men he was talking with and his hair was slightly mussed from the breeze.

She put on her best smile of apology as she approached him. "Gannon, sorry I'm . . . I'm . . ." When he turned at the sound of his name, her heart lurched oddly in her chest at the sight of his smile. Her voice trailed off. She felt an unexpected vacuum in her midriff that stole all the breath from her lungs. How could she have forgotten how astoundingly good-looking he was? He wore tan chinos and a blue shirt with the sleeves rolled over his powerful forearms. The knot in his tie was loose and the top button of his shirt was undone. A tan sport coat, hooked on two fingers, was slung casually over his shoulder. She had barely gotten her breath back before his welcoming smile warmed her and his arms opened.

She went into them without the least hesitation or thought for their audience, tilting her head up for his kiss.

"I missed you so damn much," he murmured, his lips only a fraction of an inch away from hers. "Thanks for meeting me." Then his mouth came crashing down, hungry and hauntingly intimate, familiar in a way that surprised her, almost as though they'd kissed every day of their lives.

She was rocked by the sensation. Her fingers clenched in the fabric of his shirt, opened to smooth at the muscular chest beneath and finally reached for the strong column of his neck.

When he stopped the kiss she wanted to protest. Instead she put her face into the hollow formed by his jaw and shoulder and inhaled the masculine scent of him. She was surprised, too, by the shivers of desire that sprang from where his hard torso fused with hers, making their way through her body, awakening each of her nerves.

Gannon seemed to sense her reaction and her surprise. He chuckled softly. "Wouldn't it be better if we finished this someplace less public?" he asked gently, his breath warm against her temple.

She nodded, looking around. The two men Richard had been standing with had drifted away. "I guess so." But she didn't move out of his arms.

His voice was just the least bit shaky. "Honey, in about two seconds you're going to melt my socks off."

Lauren laughed softly under his chin. Suddenly she was happy with the bubbling happiness that stirred the bloodstream and made the top of her head seem light. "Just your socks? That wouldn't do much good, would it?" She lifted her head to look up at him. "Unless you have a foot fetish," she suggested, a teasing glint in her dark blue eyes.

"I love every inch of you. You might be quite shocked at some of the fetishes I've dreamed about since you said you'd marry me," he warned her huskily.

Marry. Oh, Lord, she'd forgotten to tell her mother about the wedding. She'd better explain. Reluctantly she pulled free of his arms and took his hand, intent on leading him to the Jeep. "Come on. We have to talk on the way home."

He didn't move, and she found herself stopped after only two steps by the firm grip of his hand. He pulled her back until she was inches from him. "Lauren? You are still going to marry me, aren't you?" His tanned features seemed to have suddenly gone pale. His gray eyes were shuttered, his expression guarded.

"Of course I am."

Richard felt himself relax, felt the surge of relief ease the foreboding that had gripped him like a huge hand squeezing his heart. There it was again—the suspicion that something was not right. "Then you haven't told your parents about us?"

"Yes, I've told them. They're very pleased." She dropped her head, kicking the grass with a sandal-clad toe. "I just haven't told them when."

He was puzzled, and still wary. "Look at me," he commanded, and she complied. "Why not?" he asked.

Lauren studied him for a moment. His expression was faintly detached, sending a chill of disappointment through her. Though she'd seen that look only rarely, she hated it. It was the look he showed to strangers. "Let me ask you something first. Do you want a big to-do at our wedding?"

The detachment faded. "No!" he said immediately. "All I want is you."

"I don't, either. But my mother is an organizer. She's already started making lists and plans, and she probably thinks that we won't get married for at least a year. Can you imagine what it would be like if I told her we were marrying at the end of the month?"

Richard grinned, overwhelmed with relief. "Would you rather elope?"

"No. That would break their hearts. But I really don't want a huge wedding like my sister had. It was a nightmare. I just decided it might be easier to tell them if you were with me. Maybe they'd think . . ."

The grin widened in understanding. "That I was rushing you because I'm so impatient to get you into my bed permanently?"

"Something like that," she admitted. "What do you think? Will it work?"

He pretended to ponder. Then, laughing, he threw an arm across her shoulder and reached for his suitcase. "Ah, babe. Convincing them of that will be a snap, because I am extremely impatient." His voice dropped suggestively on the last sentence. "This may have been the longest week of my life. Lead me to them."

The husky timbre in his voice and his warm breath at her ear brought on another wave of weakness in Lauren's knees. They had reached the hood of the Jeep, and she had to put out a hand to steady herself. Without a doubt, Richard's acting this way and her obvious physical response to him ought to give her parents peace of mind. As for her, she wasn't sure. Only a short while ago she'd been lecturing herself about the importance of meeting life and marriage with a practical outlook.

"You smell wonderful," he murmured into her hair.

Her knees wobbled again. With a fist under her chin he raised her face for another brief kiss. "I want to be alone with you, darling," he whispered. "I want to kiss you mindless, and without an audience. Where's the car?"

Unable to tear her eyes from his, she swallowed and patted the hood under her hand. "R-right here."

Finally he released her gaze. "This?" He seemed surprised but pleased, seeing the old vehicle.

Lauren found climbing into the Jeep more of an effort than it had ever been before. She watched as Richard tossed his bag into the back and circled the vehicle. As he climbed in beside her, she decided it was definitely time to lighten the atmosphere. "There is one other thing I should warn you about," she said, smiling, her hand on the ignition key.

Gannon turned in the seat and let his arm rest on the back behind Lauren's head. The teasing light in her eyes, her warm smile told him that this was something he could handle. "Let's have it."

"My father is scared to death that he's going to have to listen to all sorts of stuff about how you plan to take care of me and what your prospects are. Before my sister married, her fiancé had Daddy in the study for half a day. Lynne's husband is rather an earnest young man, you see. When Daddy came out he told me—in confidence, of course—that he was awfully afraid Lynne wouldn't live to see thirty. She'd be bored to death within a year."

"I think I'm going to like your father," Richard said with a smile.

"COME IN. COME IN," said Sarah from the top step of the porch. Flanked by her husband and the butler, she held out both hands. "We're so happy to welcome you to our home, Richard. And to the family."

Without being instructed, Shaw went to the Jeep to unload Richard's bag. He disappeared with it.

Richard paused on the step below the elder Wildings, uttering a silent groan. Her mother's welcome was genuine, but Red Wilding, while not openly hostile, was clearly reserving judgment. Well, what did he expect? He knew the man's reputation for being a hard-nosed businessman. "Thank you, Mrs. Wilding. It's nice to be here." He took her hands in his and bent over one of them with smooth urbanity.

"Please call me 'Sarah.'"

Richard nodded. "Thank you, Sarah." He turned to Lauren's father. "Mr. Wilding."

"Gannon," said Red tersely, shaking the hand that Richard extended to him. "Good to have you here."

They moved into an entrance hall of large proportions. Richard saw at once that his fiancée was her father's daughter. Lauren probably didn't even realize that she automatically gravitated to her father's side. He felt a sudden resentment at her defection, then silently chided himself for his jealousy.

"We can't stand around all afternoon." Sarah finally scolded pleasantly. "Lauren, you take Richard up to his room. Richard, I hope Lauren has told you about the Courtlands' party tonight and that we have to dine early because of it. I'm sorry we must rush so. Lauren, do you have Richard's tie? We'll meet on the patio for drinks in an hour. Come along, Will." Sarah never called her husband by the nickname "Red." She hated it.

"Where have you put Richard, Mother?" Lauren stemmed the tide long enough to ask.

"In Lynne's old room, darling," her mother answered with an innocent smile.

Red Wilding grunted something disapproving under his breath, but before he could make his objections audible Sarah packed him off to the patio—to ply him with fine bourbon, if Lauren wasn't mistaken.

"What was all that about?" asked Richard as he followed her up a broad curving staircase.

She peeped over the banister to make sure that her parents were out of earshot before she answered. "We're sharing a bath. Daddy probably thinks that's decadent. He's a bit old-fashioned where his daughters are concerned. This way."

"Doesn't your mother share his attitude?"

Lauren gave him a provocative smile over her shoulder. "Oh, no. Mother's a romantic to the bone. She put you there on purpose."

His eyes turned the color of old silver and he reached for her, but she laughed and, skipping a step, neatly avoided his outstretched hand. Taking a left at the top of the stairs, she led him through an arched opening into a wide hall.

Richard looked around. The hall was furnished as a sitting room, with plush sofas and easy chairs upholstered in bright chintzes. A stereo took up one section of a ceiling-high bookcase, but the rest of its shelves were filled with everything from Emerson to Vonnegut to tempt the reader.

"Lynne and I had these two rooms when we were growing up," she said, indicating the doors to their right. "The boys were across the hall. And there's a playroom and a small kitchen at the end there. But when Lynne married and started having children, mother had to move her to the other side to have room for them all when she visits."

"How many children does she have?"

"Three. And she's pregnant again. Daddy doesn't think Patrick knows what causes them."

"Or maybe sex is the only thing that doesn't bore her to death."

Lauren flushed guiltily. "I shouldn't have said that. Patrick is a very nice man, and he loves Lynne and the children to distraction." Her eyes took on a wistful cast. "I would love to see the babies. It doesn't seem the same without Lynne and her family here, but the doctor wouldn't let her travel."

Richard was taken by the setting, thinking how nice it would be to grow up here with a loving family and security to soften the blows of adolescence. "Where do your brothers stay when they come, now that Lynne and her brood have taken over their rooms?"

"Slade stays in whichever room happens to be empty. Marshall has a summer home here. Years ago Daddy gave each of us a parcel of land to build on when we marry."

He lifted a dark brow. "You have one, too?"

"Yes, ten acres on the lake." Her eyes sparkled at the thought that next year when the family gathered she might have a place of her own. Might even be pregnant! "Come on, you can see from your window." She opened a door on her right. "This is your room. You don't have to fight ruffles and lace. Mother had it all redone." She hurried across to open the drapes. Richard followed more slowly, looking around at the pleasant room.

It was decorated in natural colors, terra cotta and forest green, and the furniture was comfortable. In addition to the king-size bed, there were deep upholstered pieces in a semicircle facing the fireplace, convenient tables and a large desk placed in front of the windows. He dropped his coat on a copy of Waller's *Saratoga, Saga of an Impious Era,* which had been placed on the bench at the foot of the bed.

"Can you see the headland just beyond the grove of pines?"

He came up behind her and followed the direction of her finger. The lake was probably two miles away but fully visible because of the elevation of this house, evidently built on the highest point on the property. The lake water sparkled blue and clear in the late-afternoon sunlight, and the pastoral scene was like an impressionist painting, its lines blurred, peaceful and serene. "Very beautiful," he agreed softly. "Can we walk over and see it?"

"I'll take you over tomorrow. Slade's and Lynne's lots are on either side. Lynne and Patrick can't afford to build yet—high school chemistry teachers aren't renowned for being wealthy." Richard felt sympathy for the unknown Patrick. A high school teacher among the high-powered, ambitious Wildings must feel out of place, to say the least.

Lauren turned in time to catch the drift of his thoughts from his expression. "Yes, he does feel overwhelmed occasionally. But he can hold his own," she said in defense of her brother-in-law. "He chose his profession because he loves kids."

Richard held up his hands, palms out. "I didn't say a word," he protested.

"But I knew what you were thinking."

His eyes narrowed in mock horror. "Oh-oh. I think I'm in big trouble if you've learned to read my mind already."

Lauren laughed and moved away. "The dressing room's through there," she said, indicating a door in the opposite wall. "And here's the bath. It connects our rooms." Lauren heard her own chattering, and almost groaned aloud. But she couldn't subdue the sudden sense of anticipation that had seized her at the thought of being married, having children, building a house on her land . . . being married. Good Lord, where was her objectivity? Ever since the kiss at the airport she realized that she physically wanted this man, wanted him with an intensity she'd never expected to feel.

A thoughtful Richard followed Lauren through a large bathroom to her room beyond. And was completely surprised. He had never considered the possibility that she was the ruffles type, but this was an old-fashioned room if he ever saw one. A four-poster was covered in blue and white gingham and canopied in white eyelet. White curtains were draped and tied away from the windows. The blue and white lamps on the bedside tables were certainly delft.

"I really should do some redecorating in here, too," she said, noticing his amazement. She looked around, seeing her room through his eyes, and made a face. "It looks like it belongs to a sixteen-year-old, doesn't it?"

"I like it," he said immediately. "It gives me insight into another side of you."

Lauren wasn't sure she wanted him to have too many insights. She kept repeating to herself that if this marriage was to succeed it should be based on practical things like respect and admiration. And their separate identities would have to be maintained. Too much knowledge of each other could threaten their independence.

She kept repeating those things to herself, but they were useless, rote observations. Her mind was occupied almost totally with the broad shoulders and narrow waist, the strength of his thighs under his chinos and the rough thatch of hair visible at the open neck of his shirt.

Get yourself under control. She deliberately turned toward her window. "Come over here and I'll familiarize you with the layout of the house." She pointed. "The pool is in the opposite wing, there where the arched openings are. And the tennis courts are behind the big hedge. If you want to ride we keep a few pleasure horses in the stables. My brother Slade can show you the best trails, but he won't be here until next weekend."

Richard gave a sigh of resignation and came up behind her, wrapping his arms around her shoulders to pull her back against his chest. "Lauren, relax. I'm not going to pounce on you," he said, completely misunderstanding her sudden agitation.

"I know," she admitted quietly. "But I'm feeling rather strange. I may pounce on you."

Richard felt his heart give a strong leap in his chest. This was so out of character for the woman he'd put on the train last week that he was surprised all over again. He forced his voice to remain level, but he couldn't keep the laughter out of it. "Do you think I'll protest?"

She shook her head, smiling. The scent of her hair, released by the movement, anesthetized him for a minute. It was French, musky and totally sensual. He put his face against the silky strands and breathed deeply.

She turned in his arms to face him, her hands resting lightly on his chest. "Oh, Richard. It's going to be a good marriage, isn't it?" she whispered.

He wondered if she felt the rapid beat of his heart under them as his eyes roamed over her beloved features. Her lips were parted enough for him to have a glimpse of her pink tongue. His breathing quickened as he focused on it. "It's going to be the best," he breathed. He bent his head slowly, relishing the anticipation of a taste, when all of a sudden the door was flung open with a force that sent it crashing against the wall. "Aunt Lauren! We're here!"

Lauren let her forehead fall forward to rest against his chest for a moment. Then she raised her head to smile apologetically at him.

Richard's mouth curved into a wry grin. "It seems we have company."

"You're about to meet the heir apparent. It will get worse," she predicted, holding out her arms to the rusty-haired child of about ten who threw himself at her, and the older boy who followed. Richard wondered at the sarcastic edge to her voice.

Marshall and Regina Wilding entered the room on the heels of their offspring. In looks Marshall was the most like Lauren and her mother, but his eyes lacked the lively sparkle of the two. His wife was a handsome, if thin-lipped woman who wore propriety like a cloak.

Richard shook hands with both of them and gained for himself what he presumed were their gayest smiles.

He could almost see the questions poised on Regina Wilding's tongue as her eyes went from Richard to Lauren.

Lauren put out a hand to him, which he clasped securely. She gave him a grateful glance and hung on as she made the introductions. The redheaded whirlwind was Wally; the older boy, Chip. When she said the word *fiancé* all four pairs of eyes converged on him.

"Fiancé! Why didn't you tell anyone?" asked Marshall. "Be quiet, children. Or did you tell everyone but me?"

"No, dear brother. You are the first. And I'm counting on you to keep the others out of my hair."

Regina was shaking Richard's free hand, and now she studied him more closely. He felt as though he were a particularily interesting bug under a microscope. "You must be some man if you've managed to snare Marshall's sister into a promise of matrimony. Of course, I'll believe it when I see it."

"Regina!" Even Marshall obviously didn't approve of the blunt statement.

Richard smiled blandly at her cynicism. "I plan to hold her to the promise," he said, and Regina nodded.

"Well, it's certainly exciting news. I must say we think it's about time Lauren settled down. We've been telling her so for years. Congratulations."

"Thank you," said Richard gravely, trying to hide a grin. He wondered if that was a royal "we." He decided that these two might constitute the reason for Lauren's reticence to announce their engagement before he arrived to provide support. And for the hint of sarcasm in Regina's voice. He could imagine the discourses Lauren had probably been subjected to over the years. Regina seemed the type to deliver a lecture at the drop of a hat.

Lauren caught the almost supressed smile on Richard's face. She squeezed his hand . . . hard. "Ah, but Richard was worth waiting for. Don't you agree?"

When the boys had gotten their share of Lauren's attention, their mother sent them to the playroom and the four adults moved out into the wide hall and settled into chairs.

Regina, it seemed, had a world of gossip to fill Lauren in on. Lauren looked more resigned than interested, but put a polite smile on her face. Richard smiled and gave Marshall the international look of masculine understanding when confronted with women who have a lot to say to each other. The look was met with a blank stare.

After a few minutes of stilted talk Richard had achieved a degree of friendliness from Marshall that was adequate, if not enthusiastic. He was surprised at the extreme difference between this eldest son and the other members of the family he'd met. Even Red Wilding, who had yet to be won over, wasn't stiff-necked. He wondered what kind of man Slade Wilding was.

The conversation might have gone on and on had Sarah not interrupted. "Children, you cannot sit around talking any longer," she said briskly as she entered the hall. "It will soon be time for supper." She was carrying a handful of brightly colored ties. "Here's one for you Marshall and you, Richard."

Richard looked questioningly at the oblong of silk that Sarah had draped over his fingers. Marshall held his up to glare at it distastefully. Both ties were a brilliant shade of lavender.

Lauren laughed at Richard's expression and stood to link her arm through his. "Mrs. Courtland chooses a color scheme for the party and the ladies are expected to dress in that color," she explained, trying to hide her grin. The gentlemen may wear their dinner clothes, but they have to wear a tie of the same color."

Richard stared at her in amazement for a minute. "You're kidding." Then he turned to Marshall. "Tell me she's kidding."

"I'm afraid she's not." Marshall still wore the same look of long-suffering disgust. "Repulsive, isn't it?"

Richard decided that stiff-necked or not, he believed he could relate to his future brother-in-law.

3

RED WILDING pulled the ancient Deusenberg up to the entrance of the three-story structure. Lights blazed from every window. The Canfield Casino, now serving as a museum for one of the most extravagant yet fascinating eras in American history, was a tribute to romantic names and tales out of the past that excited the imagination—Diamond Jim Brady and Lillian Russell, eating their way through gargantuan meals; Florenz Ziegfeld and lovely Anna Held, his Parisian discovery, later his wife; Nellie Bly, who "exposed" Saratoga's wickedness in her feminist writing for the *New York World*.

Lauren bit back a groan when she saw the reporters milling around the entrance. Richard caught the sound and squeezed her hand. "Another insight into your personality."

"I don't know what you mean."

"I mean you're insecure when you have to face the press . . . or is it crowds?"

"Nonsense!" She tried to keep her laugh light.

The reporters were out in force tonight, vying for a word, a picture of the motion picture personalities, television stars and other celebrities who usually gathered for the occasion. The very visible Mrs. Courtland had decreed that the members of the media were welcome to cover her annual party until nine o'clock. At that time they were to disappear, leaving the rich and famous to their fun.

"C'mon, Wilding. I've got nail marks on my hand."

She looked down, contrite, to see that he was telling the truth. "I'm sorry, Richard." She tugged at her hand, but he refused to release her.

"I wasn't complaining, merely making an observation."

"Okay," she relented, smiling. "I do like my privacy."

"So do I. Do you think we might find some of it later?"

Lauren laughed, and just then the young parking attendant approached the car.

Her father set the brake of the vehicle. He gave a warning glare to the uniformed boy. "Do you know how to drive this thing, son?"

"Yes, sir! She'll be as safe with me as a jug of moonshine with a mountain man on Saturday night." The young man flashed him a grin. He opened the door and gallantly assisted Sarah as she stepped down from the running board of the high vehicle.

"Why am I not reassured?" grumbled Red.

Richard chuckled, extending his hand to Lauren. Pride mingled with awe as he helped her from the back seat of the old convertible. Beautiful women were the

norm in his circles, but this beautiful woman out-
classed all the others he'd ever known.

She might have stepped from the pages of the original *Vanity Fair*. In the theme of the party, she wore a
twenties-style gown in a soft shade of beaded lavender crepe. Cut straight across her breasts, the dress
was held up with tiny shimmering straps. It ended at
her knees with a border of fringe that flipped and
parted to show a glimpse of thigh with each step. She
wore pearls that were almost as long as the dress itself, and her shining cap of hair was circled with a
matching beaded band.

Richard silently blessed Sarah Wilding for giving
them connecting rooms.

Sarah was dressed in chiffon, a darker shade of the
lavender. While Lauren let the wind blow through her
hair freely, Sarah had chosen a turban for protection
in the open car. The intricately folded fabric sported
a jaunty curled feather.

He didn't hear the imprecation his fiancée muttered under her breath as they approached the reporters, but it was quite clear from the movement of
her lips that she had said a word that was definitely
unladylike. "Miss Wilding!" he teased in a whisper.

"Sorry," she muttered.

If Lauren was uncomfortable, she was also determined that no one would know. She smiled brightly
for the cameras and tightened her grip on Richard's
arm. He covered her fingers reassuringly with his own
as they mounted the steps.

"Miss Wilding! Lauren! Won't you introduce us to your escort?"

Any minute now, any minute, Lauren thought, one of these reporters was going to recognize Richard; then the speculation would begin. But to her surprise it didn't seem to bother him. He simply grinned, lifted his hand in casual greeting for the cameras and adroitly maneuvered them through the press without ever saying a word. Only when they had reached the top of the steps did she hear a voice behind them say, "That's Richard Gannon!"

When they reached the double doors they were halted by a crowd of people jammed just inside. She smiled up at him. "That was very smooth."

"I'm an old hand," he murmured with just a trace of resignation in his voice. His hand slid to her waist.

She smiled. "I'll bet you are, being Bachelor of the Year and all."

"Not for long," he growled under his breath, and brought her closer in a brief hug. "But even a day is too long for me. I like the way this dress looks on you, by the way."

Lauren was surprised to find that with Richard, flirting came quite naturally. "And how *does* it look?" she asked provocatively.

He gave her a wolfish smile. "It just skims your body, barely touching the—" his gaze dropped to her breasts "—important parts."

What began as a laugh became a catch of her breath in response to the promising warmth in his voice. Her pulse sped up, sending a flood of expectancy racing through her bloodstream. "I shouldn't have asked."

Sarah and Red came up behind them, interrupting the spell that kept their gazes locked. "Come on, come on," said Red. "Let's find our table."

Richard's lips curved in a frustrated half smile that Lauren understood. "Yes, Daddy," she said automatically, still entranced by Richard's smoky, sensual eyes.

"Well, move on, Lauren," Red repeated.

The hand at her waist moved restlessly, shifting the beaded fabric against her skin in an soft abrasiveness that was very erotic in light of his comment. Her parents were right behind them. He couldn't say anything without being overheard. But words were unnecessary; his eyes spoke volumes. Tonight, they said. Tonight, her expression clearly agreed.

Red cleared his throat loudly. "There are people in back of us who wish to enjoy the party from the inside," he said in a booming voice that sent warmth rushing up to color Lauren's cheeks. Richard offered Sarah a look of apology, but she simply smiled her pleasure.

To Richard the inside of the casino seemed to be utter chaos at first. He'd heard of the party, of course. Everyone had heard of the party, but he was unprepared for the scope of it.

The vast, European-style dining room was decorated to resemble a luxurious speakeasy. A band was doing its level best to encourage the theme with an enthusiastic rendition of "Yes, Sir, That's My Baby." A few couples were already on the dance floor, moving in a ragged version of the Charleston. A manmade pavilion had been constructed in the center of the room as a background from which the hostess welcomed her guests. Exotic orchid plants swung gently in the breeze from a ceiling fan inside. Huge jungle ferns, higher than even Richard's head, formed a frame for the diminutive Mrs. Courtland. She looked like an exquisite hothouse blossom herself, greeting them over the noise of the orchestra.

"Lauren, dear, it's wonderful to see you." Mary Ann Courtland took Lauren's hands and kissed the air beside her cheek. She turned to Richard. "And this is . . . ?"

"This is Richard Gannon. Richard, Mary Ann Courtland."

"Of course. I've heard of you. So glad you could come, Richard. Lauren, show him around. I'll see you both later."

Lauren took Richard's hand. "For a donation," she told him under her breath. "Did you bring your checkbook?"

He grinned. "As a matter of fact, I did. What charity is she sponsoring?"

"I'm not sure. Last year it was the Olympics—or was that year before last? Come on."

Richard spoke into her ear. "This is quite a show."

Lauren shook her head, smiling up at him. "Isn't it something? You know every year I vow I'm not going to come to this party. Even if it is for a good cause, it's a circus. But it's irresistible."

She pointed to a large group in one corner of the ballroom. "That crowd over there is waiting to make their own ice cream sundaes." Models and movie stars, titans of the theater and television personalities—people who would kick the scale if it showed a spare ounce, who would automatically expect exemplary service in a fine restaurant—clustered like birds at a feeder, waiting to manufacture for themselves a sticky, dripping concoction loaded with a month's worth of extra calories. In another corner a high chef's hat bobbled as a man took orders for specialty omelets. His expertise was part of the show.

"What happened to Mother and Daddy?"

"There they are." Richard indicated the direction with a nod.

Lauren took a look at the table for eight where her parents and Marshall and Regina had been joined by her father's sister and brother. The surrounding tables were also filled with her relatives. "Take a long breath and polish up your photographic memory, Gannon. You're going to need it." Hands still entwined, they made their way through the crowd.

Half an hour later he was beginning to wonder if Lauren was related to everyone in the room. When they finally sat down, he asked.

She responded with a laugh. "Only half of them."

"By blood, the other half she's related to by marriage," put in Red Wilding's elder sister, a dowager type seated on Richard's left. "Lauren, why don't you rescue this nice young man? Go dance or something."

"Of course, Aunt Mattie. Will you dance with me, darling?"

"Not until that song is over, darling," Richard responded dryly. "If you saw me try to Charleston, you'd call off the engagement immediately."

Before she could remonstrate a man came up behind her chair and said, "Lauren? Are they playing our song?"

She twisted to see who was kissing the back of her neck. "Cuffy!" She stood, hugged the young blond Adonis enthusiastically. "Of course they are! But first I want you to meet—" Before she could complete the statement she was pulled unceremoniously away from the table. She threw a helpless smile at Richard, who had risen to his feet. He watched, a frown across his brow.

Aunt Mattie touched his arm. "Sit down, Richard. He's an old friend of the family."

"I wasn't—"

"Of course you weren't," she kindly finished for him. "Three-forths of the men under forty in this room have proposed to Lauren at one time or another, but she chose you. So there's no reason to be jealous."

A voice screeched from behind him. "Richard!"

Richard got to his feet again, just in time to catch the lovely brunette who hurled herself at him. "Hello, Darlene," he said, grimacing inwardly. Darlene Hudson, a producer at Radio City Music Hall in New

York, had enjoyed a brief place in his life several years ago. He introduced her to the others at the table.

Darlene nodded perfunctorily, but she was more interested in him. "What are you doing here, sweetie?"

Embarrassed by the endearment, Richard smiled weakly at his future in-laws. Red and Marshall scowled; Sarah and Aunt Mattie looked pleased. He offered Darlene his chair, but she shook her head.

"Can't stay now." She curled her arm around his neck and pulled his head down for a long kiss. Short of dumping her in the floor, there was no way to avoid those heavily glossed lips. "I'm at the Renaissance. Call me," she said in a suggestive tone. "We'll get together."

When she was gone, he sank gratefully into his chair, only to pop up again as Cuffy returned Lauren to her party and left. The minute Richard saw Lauren's narrowed gaze he knew she had seen the kiss. "An old friend," he offered.

"She left her mark."

For a minute he didn't understand what she meant. Then her eyes dropped to his mouth. Hastily he pulled out his handkerchief and wiped away the red stain. "Did I get it all?" he asked innocently.

The dimple played in her cheek for a minute. "Yes. But I think it's about time for the engagement announcement to go in the papers, don't you?"

"Definitely," he agreed without missing a beat. "Tomorrow?"

She laughed lightly. "Even you couldn't accomplish it that quickly."

Suddenly Richard was serious. "Do you doubt it?" he asked in a low voice.

She studied him for a minute. "I don't think I dare doubt you. Shall we wake up the editor of the *Philadelphia Enquirer*?"

"You wouldn't have to," put in Sarah blandly. "He's over there with Mary Ann, dancing the Charleston. Will, darling, the man's ten years older than you, and look at him. Why can't you dance like that?"

Red's look was sour. "Because I don't have two left feet," he retorted, obviously pleased with his own quick wit.

Lauren noticed that even Marshall seemed to be infected with enthusiasm tonight. He filled glasses with wine and passed them around. "Here you go, Gannon. Shall we drink to your coming nuptials?"

Lauren laughingly accepted a glass. "Nuptials? Marshall, how much wine have you had?"

"Seems a fitting way to describe it amid all this." He indicated the room with a careless wave. "Come to think of it, we should be drinking bathtub gin. Everybody got a glass? Okay. Here's to my sister Lauren and her fiancé, Richard Gannon."

In the way of all the contrariest laws of nature, there was a sudden moment of total silence into which Marshall's last six words fell like stones.

Lauren's gaze sought Richard's and they shared the same thought. If only they'd had a little more private time together.

Richard grinned and shrugged. There was an immediate deluge of well-wishers at their table. Richard found that he knew a good percentage of them. A young accountant he'd hired three months ago was here with her parents. He could almost hear her broadcasting the news in the offices of Gannon Consultants on Monday morning.

An hour later Richard finally managed to get Lauren all to himself for a few minutes. True, they were in the middle of a crowded dance floor, but the wild and jazzy music had changed to a slow, dreamy foxtrot and he was shooting daggers at any man who even looked as if he might cut in.

"How long does this go on?" he growled in her ear. "I want very much to get you alone." His lips strayed over her forehead as he added whimsically, "It seems to me I've said those words before."

Lauren nestled her head under his chin, liking the way they fitted together, liking the scent of his cologne, liking the strength of his arms. "Marshall and Regina will be the first to leave. We can ride with them."

"Good. I have something to give you, but I refuse to do it until we're alone."

"Hi, Richard," a soft voice intruded.

Richard lifted his head to look at the couple dancing off to their right. He didn't know the man, but his partner was another former girlfriend. Good Lord, he thought despairingly, the place was filled with them. "Hello, Pattie. How are you?"

"Fine," the tiny blond said. "Congratulations. I just heard you're getting married." She smiled a bit sadly. "Hi, Lauren."

Richard felt Lauren move restlessly in his arms, and then she returned the greeting shortly. "Hi, Pattie."

When the other couple had danced away, she tilted her head back to look up at him. She didn't seem pleased. "Lord, Gannon, am I going to be stumbling over your old friends every time I turn around?"

Richard made a sudden decision. "Let's get out of here. I'll get a cab."

"That's a good idea. We need to discuss a few things," Lauren agreed briskly.

He gave her a sharp look. The sweet, rather dreamy expression she had worn at the start of the evening had totally disappeared.

THE HOUSE BLAZED with light, but their footsteps rang hollowly as they mounted the staircase. A lamp cast a soft glow over the sitting area in the upstairs hall-way of the children's wing. Since no one else was staying in this side of the house, Lauren decided that perhaps it would be better to have their discussion here rather than in either of the bedrooms.

She was not a jealous person, but tonight had brought home to her just how popular with the women Richard was. His appeal to women had been obvious from the first, but lately—since she had been the center of his attention—she'd either forgotten it or put it out of her mind.

If this marriage was to get off to a good start there shouldn't be any misunderstanding between them about their expectations. She paused long enough to flip on the stereo to a favorite FM radio station. The rules should be clarified. The problem was, she wasn't sure how to make certain things clear to him without giving herself away. She knew what she wanted from this marriage, but what did Richard want? And how much was either of them willing to give?

"Shaw put some brandy out for us. How nice. May I pour you one?" she asked, going to the mahogany sideboard that held the tray. This was not going to be an easy conversation and she needed something to fortify her.

He took off his dinner jacket and tossed it over a chair before joining her. "If you're having one." He pulled at the offensive lavender tie and dropped it beside the tray. He undid one of the onyx studs of his fine linen shirt, then another.

All of this Lauren saw in the periphery of her vision. Splashing some of the dark liquid into both of the bubble glasses, she handed one to him.

"Thanks." He opened a third button.

Dragging her eyes away from the vee of skin shadowed by dark hair, she bent to open one of the drawers. "I'm sure there are some napkins here somewhere." She swept her hair away from her face and tilted her head to look. "Here they are."

Suddenly she was being held by her elbow and swung around to face him. "I don't give a damn about a napkin or the brandy." He disposed of the glass he was holding, leaned against the chest and pulled her close between his thighs. "All I really want to taste is you." He slid the headband off her hair and dropped it on the surface behind him beside his tie.

The tight ribbon of beads had left a pink mark on her forehead. He touched his lips there and stroked the spot with his thumbs, smiling slightly. "You've played the twenties vamp to the hilt tonight, sweetheart." His hands plunged into her hair, lifting the strands to let them sift between his fingers like golden threads of silk. "And I'm panting." His mouth came down to cover hers in a soft kiss that asked, that persuaded . . . that finally demanded.

"Richard, wait. We really need to talk," Lauren said breathlessly, turning her head aside. She was fighting the overwhelming urge to forget everything except the sensual draw of this man.

"Later."

"No." Her hands pushed against his chest insistently. "This is important."

"So is this." When Richard finally realized he wasn't going to get the kind of response he wanted, he sighed and released her. Taking up the glass of brandy, he eyed her over its rim. "Shoot."

Lauren crossed to sit at one end of the sofa. She smoothed her hair with an apprehensive gesture. "Sit down," she ordered. "I can't think with you looming over me like that."

Richard smiled to himself at the show of nerves. She was uneasy, self-conscious. Perhaps even a little jealous after running into two of his old flames. He was surprised to find the idea intriguing. He had been the subject of jealous scenes in the past and hated it, but from the woman he loved a small dose of the emotion was rather flattering.

Mentally he shook himself. This was crazy. He didn't want Lauren to have any doubts about his love for her. It was time to give her the ring he'd selected in Amsterdam, to let her know she was the only woman in the world for him.

"Pattie is a beautiful woman," she began.

"Yes, she is."

"Darlene, too."

"Oh, yes!" He grinned and spread his hands. "Honey, I'm thirty-eight years old. You know there have been women." Then he reached into the pocket of his trousers and closed his fingers around the ring. At her next words, however, he hesitated.

Lauren took a deep breath, determined to handle this in a businesslike, civilized way. "Richard, we've never discussed . . ." She paused, searching for a better way of bringing up the subject, then plunged on. "I don't know what you expect of marriage, but I'd like to explain what I expect."

Watching her with a narrowed gaze, he withdrew his hand from his pocket, hitched his trousers and sat down slowly in a chair facing her. He knew what he wanted from marriage, but he wasn't sure what he expected from this conversation. For some reason he had a feeling he was going to be surprised. "Go on."

"Well." She linked her fingers together and leaned forward, her elbows on her knees. Her posture was a plea for him to follow her meaning. "I don't want our marriage to be a prison for you—for either of us. You travel a lot. So do I. Misunderstandings can lead to upsetting complications...I..." She was becoming completely flustered. "How do you feel about fidelity?" She finally blurted.

Richard looked at her strangely.

She rushed on. "I'm doing this badly. What I mean is, I realize men have a stronger sex drive than women. Modern open marriages might be okay for some, but not for me. If you decided to be unfaithful, Richard, I would be horribly...embarrassed."

Astonishment was a weak word for what Richard felt. He slumped against the back of the chair and stared at her. "Embarrassed?" he asked quietly. "Not betrayed? Hurt?"

"Yes. Naturally I would be hurt, too," she conceded.

Richard's thoughts were confused, wildly jumbled. He remembered his misgivings on several different occasions, his instincts trying to warn him that something was not right. He also remembered that he had ignored them. Now he had no idea what the hell was going on here.

He didn't speak for some time. When he did there was something in his voice that caused Lauren to cringe inwardly. Outwardly she remained calm.

"You were right about one thing," he grated. "You're doing this very badly, indeed." Suddenly spurred to anger, he lunged to his feet. His long legs took him down the hall away from her.

He stood with his back turned, tossing the ring absently in his hand. Richard had learned at an early age to control his temper, to harness the energy of anger and make it work for, rather than against him. Not since he was very young had he come closer to losing that control.

Lauren tried desperately to think of a way to explain further. She watched him cram his fists into his pockets, watched as he moved the powerful shoulders as though to shrug off tension. Finally he turned back.

When he spoke his voice was restrained and horribly quiet. "First let me reassure you that I have no intention of sleeping around. But I am beginning to realize that your own intentions are rather vague to me. You've told me what you don't want—suppose you tell me what it is you do want out of marriage?"

She recognized the tremendous control he was exerting over his temper. She called upon every resource to maintain her composure under his furious gaze. From the way he moved, from the jumping muscle in his strong jaw to the unconscious flexing of his muscular arms to the chilling emotion in his eyes, she knew that she had unleashed the quality that she had once suspected lurked under his polished facade, something slightly untamed.

Vaguely her mind registered the soft strains of Vivaldi coming from the stereo. Music soothes the savage breast—in most instances. This time it was up to her. She suddenly realized that she wanted very much to soothe this man.

"I want the kind of marriage that will last," she told him softly but without hesitation. "One based on friendship and common interests, affection and respect." The last was added with a wry travesty of a smile.

Richard wandered aimlessly around the perimeter of the rug, retrieving the brandy glass. "And love?" he asked softly.

Lauren inhaled. "I do love you, Richard. You have to believe that. I certainly wouldn't have gone—" She stopped, horrified by what she had let slip.

Richard's eyes narrowed as he searched her guilty expression. "Wouldn't have gone to all this trouble? Come on, Lauren. Let's have it all." He resumed his seat across from her, crossing one ankle on his knee and taking a hefty swallow of the brandy. She watched cautiously, knowing his casual mien was deceptive. The fingers that held the glass were white tipped with tension. A muscle in his neck pulsed irregularly. He was angry, really angry, and she couldn't blame him.

When she didn't answer immediately Richard went on, "I've felt from the first that something was off kilter in this relationship, but I haven't been able to put my finger on what it was," he said, his tone suspiciously mild. "Perhaps you should enlighten me."

She thought for a minute. He was demanding complete honesty. Her chin came up as she made her decision. She owed him just that. After all, she had begun this conversation with the purpose of clearing away misunderstandings before they arose. If he knew everything, if she could make him understand her motives, surely he would be reasonable. "Let me ask you something. Have you ever suspected a woman of trying to marry you for your money?"

His jaw set, he nodded stiffly.

"Me, too. A man, I mean. But it went further than suspicion." She laughed, but there was no humor in the sound. "It was years ago . . . I was young. Any of the people at the party tonight could have filled you in about Monty." Her eyes fell to her hands, clasped loosely in front of her. "To put it in a nutshell, he ordered beautifully in flawless French, then presented me with the check. My money was my main attraction—he told me so at the end."

"And you believed him." The statement was uttered with a certain amount of skepticism.

"It's not unheard of."

"What does this have to do with us?" Richard's lashes screened his eyes, masking his feelings; his inquiry now sounded offhand, almost indifferent. That, to Lauren, was worse than the anger.

"I'm thirty-one. I want a baby, children, a husband...and I don't have a lot more time to get them." She took a deep breath and let it out. "I looked for you."

"For me? I'm not sure I know what you mean."

"I mean that there were certain, er..."

Suddenly the truth dawned on Richard. Suddenly he knew the whole story of what she had done. She wanted to get married. As any good businesswoman would have done she'd weighed the options and done her homework. Love had never entered into it at all. What a fool he'd been! What a blind fool. "Criteria?" he asked brutally. He knew he was right when he saw her blanch.

"You make it sound so cold-blooded, so contrived." Which is exactly what it was, she reminded herself. How arrogant she had been! The enormity of what she'd done hit her. This was no boy that she might have finagled for a date to the school dance. This was a man and his life she'd been playing with.

Richard set his glass down carefully on his knee. "Maybe you should explain exactly what you were looking for."

Convincing him of the truth became uppermost in her mind and heart, which had begun to beat uncomfortably hard. She had to make him understand. "I was looking for intelligence and honesty, culture and sophistication, someone who was as involved as I am so he would understand the pressures of business. I wanted someone I could spend the rest of my life with, Richard. Not just someone who would stay with me until the glow wore off and then head for divorce court. I've seen those marriages. I've had that kind of love, if you want to call it that," she said bitterly. "I call it insanity. Don't you see? What we have will last because it's based on reason."

"Your definition of reason. Mine didn't enter into it. In fact—" he raised the glass to his lips and stared over the rim "—I had no choice, did I, Lauren?"

"Of course you had a choice. You might not have liked me at all."

He sipped and swallowed before he answered. "I presume that this hypothetical husband you were looking for needed to have a lot of money, as well. So he would fit into your life-style. You wouldn't want another man you'd have to keep, would you?"

Lauren closed her eyes against his sarcasm, even knowing she deserved it. But she had explained, however badly, her rationale. All she could do now was await his decision, and hope he could dredge up at least a modicum of understanding for her motives.

"And what about sex," he went on. "I suppose he had to be minimally appealing."

She stared at him helplessly. "Oh, Richard, much, much more than minimally." Her voice was a thin whisper.

"I should be flattered, shouldn't I? You've really done your homework! Isn't it strange that I don't feel flattered at all? Just extremely disillusioned." The hand that had gripped the wooden arm of the chair fell to the side and dangled there. His head rested against the back cushion. He stared at the ceiling, looking very sad, very vulnerable. His voice when he spoke again was tired. "Why did I think I could trust you, Lauren?" he said almost to himself. He put down the brandy glass.

She fought against the tears of remorse that filled her eyes. She didn't dare blink for fear of releasing them. Even at this moment, when she despised herself for hurting and humbling this magnificent man with her egotistical maneuvering, she faced him with composure. "I'm sorry, Richard. I never meant you to know."

He sighed heavily. "I almost wish I didn't."

"I would have been a good wife."

He gave a discordant laugh. "You've got a hell of a lot to learn, lady."

Her hands spread in an entreaty for him to understand. "I wanted the best man I could find," she added huskily.

"An appropriate stud, in other words, for these children you want so badly," he said fiercely as he rose to look down at her. He swept his jacket off the chair and hooked it over his shoulder. "Good night, Lauren." His expression was inscrutable. He turned toward the door of his room.

"What are you going to do?" she asked.

"Right now, I am going to bed. That might eliminate the temptation to wring your lovely neck."

She swallowed against the thick burning lump in her throat as she watched him go, but she had to know. "I mean about the engagement." The last word was a whisper.

He dragged an agitated hand through his hair and turned back to meet her wide-eyed stare. "Ah, hell, Lauren. I don't know what I'm going to do."

THE NEXT MORNING Lauren sat on the edge of her bed.
The sound of the running shower came from behind
the closed door of the bathroom, and she couldn't help
but picture Richard.... The shower stopped. She
jumped to her feet. Shoving her hands into her pockets, she began to prowl the room, from the dresser to
the window, back again to the bed.

She had dressed at dawn in jeans and a blue
gingham shirt, washed her face, combed her hair and
put on some lip gloss. Then she'd sat down to wait.
She had deliberately tried to keep her mind blank,
because when she thought about the conversation
they'd had last night and remembered their earlier
promises, she had a disgusting tendency to cry.

When the telephone rang beside her she almost
jumped out of her skin. She glanced at the clock.
8:00 A.M. Early for a Sunday morning call. "H-hello."
She had to clear her voice of traces of the tears she'd
shed.

"Miss Wilding, this is Roxy Lyons, Mr. Gannon's
secretary in Philadelphia. I apologize for calling so
early."

Lauren recognized the voice. The woman had called on several occasions over the past six months with messages from Richard. "Yes, Ms Lyons. How are you? Just a minute. I'll get Richard."

"I do need to speak to him," said the older woman. "But first, please let me tell you how happy I am for the two of you. Richard told me that you're going to be married."

"Ms . . . Roxy . . ."

"I know it hasn't been officially announced yet. I hope you don't mind that he told me. But I want you to know that I've worked for Richard for years and I've never seen him so happy. He's like a young kid."

Lauren blinked rapidly to clear her eyes. Her voice was husky. "Well, as you say, it isn't official yet." And never will be now. "Let me call Richard to the phone."

The bathroom door was still closed. Lauren hesitated before knocking firmly. Receiving no answer, she opened it tentatively, to be hit in the face by a wall of fragrant steam. She knocked again on the door leading to Richard's room.

"Come in." She pushed at the door. He was brushing his damp hair, bending his knees slightly so he could see in the low mirror. The dark tailored slacks were taut over his haunches; his black sweater molded strong biceps. His eyes met hers in the mirror. They were icy gray, cold and uncompromising.

"There's a phone call for you. Your secretary. You can take it there." She pointed to the extension and escaped from the room.

Back at her perch on her bed she quietly placed the receiver in its cradle.

The conversation was brief, for in only a minute he was at her door.

"Is everything all right?" she asked.

He shrugged. "The young boy I told you about?" He paused while she nodded in recognition. "One of my contacts thought he saw him last night. I would have had to go back this morning, anyway." Then, abruptly changing the subject, he asked, "What did you say to Roxanne?"

"Say? I don't . . ."

"Roxy is a perceptive woman, Lauren. She realized immediately that something had happened."

Lauren couldn't sustain his gaze any longer. His eyes were without the warmth, the affection she had grown used to seeing. She hadn't known how desperately she would miss those emotions. Bowing her head, she tried to remember her exact words. "I only confirmed to her that our engagement wasn't official yet."

He folded his arms across his chest and leaned against the doorjamb. "I'm not looking forward to the speculation that I'll have to face tomorrow in the office."

"I don't particularly relish it, either," she said sharply. "I've been through this before, you'll remember."

"Yes." Richard glanced down at his watch and sighed heavily. "I have to go. The plane will be landing in about fifteen minutes."

Lauren rose. "I have the keys to the Jeep. I'll take you to the airport."

"I've already called a cab."

He turned back into his room and she followed slowly. Avoiding his eyes, she wandered over to the window to look out toward the lake. "I'll explain everything to Mother and Daddy."

Richard didn't answer. His feelings were too raw. He tossed the brush into his shaving kit and zipped it. He eyed her slender back as he packed the kit in his suitcase and snapped it shut. The small sound held a note of finality.

Lauren ran a finger along the sill. "Richard, will you do one thing for me?" she asked softly.

He turned back to the dresser. "What is it?"

"Will you think about what I've said? Just for the week." Slowly she turned to watch as he straightened and met her gaze in the mirror. "You'd planned to come back next weekend, anyway. You could still see the races, and we could talk again."

Richard gripped the edge of the dresser, forcing himself not to jump at the suggestion. He'd be far better off never to see her again, and a week certainly wasn't long enough to allow him any kind of objectivity. "Let me ask you something first."

"Of course."

"What will you do now?"

She didn't understand. "Now?"

"If we don't marry, will you start to look for another husband?"

"No! Don't you know . . . realize. . . ." She dragged her fingers through her hair. Then her hand fell lifelessly to her side. "No."

He hesitated, studying her carefully for any sign of dissimulation. "All right," he said finally. "I'll think about what you've said, and call you if I decide to come next weekend."

Lauren's pulse jumped. "Thank you," she said. She wondered how she was going to explain the broken engagement to her parents. It wouldn't be easy, but it was necessary. She couldn't listen to the family talk about weddings or her mother singing Richard's praises when there was a strong doubt about whether there would be a wedding, or a Richard, in the Wilding family.

She had discovered in the small hours of the morning that she was devastated by the thought of losing him. She still wouldn't call it the kind of love that poets wrote about, but her feelings were deeper than she'd imagined. She wanted to tell him so. But that wouldn't be wise. He'd never believe her now. She'd be better off to keep her mouth shut and give him time.

He stood for a minute, indecisively gnawing on his lip. Finally he seemed to come to a decision. "Hold off talking to your parents until you hear from me. We can decide together the best way to handle this," he said crisply.

Her breath caught in her throat, and her heart swelled with hope. She deliberately squelched the feeling. He wasn't promising anything except a way for both of them to save face.

Scraping the loose change off the edge of the dresser, he dropped it into his pocket. A set of keys followed, and he reached for his watch, leaving only one item on the dresser.

Lauren almost cried aloud when she saw what he'd left there. She tried not to look, but her eyes were drawn to it. Richard didn't seem to notice. The significance of his omission caused her knees to buckle, and sad tears burned behind her eyes, but she certainly didn't intend to call his attention to the item. She straightened and her chin came up. "I'll walk down with you."

As they left the room together she couldn't resist a last look. The early morning sun streamed in through the sheer curtains to kiss the winking diamond ring.

LATE THAT NIGHT Richard stood at the window of his office, hands thrust deep in his pockets, looking out on the deserted city. Hoping to keep his mind off Lauren, he had come directly here from the airport, knowing he could always find work to do while he waited for word of Jay. The contact called to report there were no new developments. Jay had been seen, but had disappeared again. For the first time in Richard's adult life, though, his work and his company couldn't hold his interest.

His heart went out to the boy who had become like a younger brother to him over the past two years. Jay was the closest thing to family Richard possessed, and unadulterated fear surged through him at the thought of the teenager on the street. He'd find him. He had to find him.

The one thing Richard Gannon had missed in his life, and had always craved, was a permanent loving relationship. What he had found were warm, caring friendships, but no true affinity with a very special woman. There was enough of the realist in him to know his dream would be difficult to fulfill. And enough of the dreamer in him to believe it was possible.

Finding it in the high-powered, fast-paced world he lived in was problematical, however. He was quite adept, he thought cynically, at spotting the fakes, at identifying the feelings that might be taken for love but weren't love at all.

He'd made a drastic mistake when he'd put Lauren Wilding on a pedestal. He'd adored but also respected her, thinking she was everything he'd ever wanted in a wife—unique, with a warm sense of humor, smart, beautiful. He'd thought it was a miracle when she'd accepted his proposal. A laugh erupted aloud in the empty room, a humorless, disgusted laugh. A miracle, all right, he told himself—by definition an impossible event. He should have known. He was always suspicious when things went too well.

She was so damned desirable. And usually so coolly controlled. But she had responded to his kisses with a backfire that seemed to confuse her. There had to be a level of sensuality there that hadn't been touched, explored fully. Not yet. He had lovingly anticipated adding to her sweet confusion.

He had needs, very strong needs, and they weren't all physical. But in the six months since he'd met Lauren, those natural needs had become uncomfortably strong. He could hardly remember what a hot shower felt like. The only other thing that had saved his sanity was the frequent travel and pressure of his job. He was often too exhausted to do more than fall into bed each night, anyway.

All that should have changed last night. He gave another harsh laugh. It came out more like a sob. Hearing the ugly sound echo in the empty office, he was grateful that no one was around to witness his frustration. Blinking against the burning behind his eyes, he propped an elbow on the window frame at shoulder height and put his fist to his mouth to muffle any further sounds. *Stay angry*, he commanded himself. *Keep the anger going. It's the only emotion that might dull this terrible pain.*

He took a long, deep breath and squared his shoulders against the unseen weight there. He'd considered calling the wedding off immediately, but after a long, sleepless night trying to convince himself it was the best thing to do, he'd taken one look at her pale cheeks, her red-rimmed eyes, and held his tongue. The sight had startled him. Any sign of vulnerability was rare with Lauren. He wasn't sure whether the traces of sorrow were because her plans had failed or because she genuinely regretted her actions, but they'd touched him, and he'd agreed to think about the situation as she'd asked.

Now he regretted the impulse. The hurt was too strong. A clean break would have been less painful.

ON MONDAY Richard called Lydia Hampton and asked her to have dinner with him. Before he met Lauren he had been seeing Lydia on a regular basis. The evening was less than a success, as she told him when he took her home at ten o'clock and left her at her door.

Later that night he stood in the same position at the window of his office, still hurting, his thoughts massed in a cloud of confusion. Rain blurred the windowpane, the lights beyond, the silhouette of the city. He knew his judgment was blurred just that way by his emotions. He needed to step back to get an objective view, but he wasn't sure it was possible to step away from this situation.

He'd known from the first that Lauren's feelings weren't as strong as his own. He simply hadn't known the reason. He'd been prepared to expend the time and patience to make her love him as intensely as he loved her. So why were things any different now that her motives were out in the open?

Maybe it was time to change his strategy. He hadn't pushed her for either an emotional commitment or a physical one. But perhaps the time had come to help her down off the pedestal.

Lauren was too much a woman of today to tolerate caveman tactics, though he supposed he could take an earthier approach and see what happened. Hell, who was he kidding? He still wanted her more than any woman he'd ever known. But not at the expense of his pride.

By Wednesday the weather had cleared and Richard had decided to go back to Saratoga Springs. He couldn't explain to himself why. But—resolution firmed his jaw as he made the decision—this time they would do things his way.

His cloudy gaze cleared as he studied the rooftops beyond the immediate downtown area. He had deliberately chosen this office for himself so he would never forget. In the distance he could make out the uneven crumbling brick, the shoddy tar paper roofing. He'd overcome tremendous odds to get where he was today. He would never have done it if he'd given up when disappointments had blocked his way. The question that continued to haunt him, though, was whether he was ready to give up on Lauren.

"If there's nothing else, I'm on my way."

The voice of his secretary drew his impassive gaze to the door for a second. Then he turned away again. "Nothing else, Roxy. See you in the morning."

"Richard . . . is there . . . can I help?"

He hadn't lied when he'd told Roxanne two weeks ago that she was his best friend, and she knew him too well. It would have been impossible for him to hide from her the fact that something was bothering him, but even more impossible to explain what that something was. He would trust her with his life, but not with this information. He might see pity in her eyes, and the one emotion he would not tolerate was pity.

"There's nothing you can do to help. Thanks, anyway, Roxy."

The answer was the same one he'd given her on Monday, when she'd arrived at work to find a very different Richard from the one who'd left for Saratoga on Saturday. She knew him well enough to realize he wouldn't tell her what was bothering him. Now she hesitated only a minute, and left.

Richard sat down in his leather swivel chair and reached for the telephone. He didn't even have to think twice to recall the unlisted number.

"Hello?"

Richard squeezed his eyes shut against the pain of hearing her voice. Hell! He didn't have to put himself through this. He wouldn't go. There were plenty of women in the world. No matter if their motives were less than pure; Lauren's weren't exactly beyond reproach.

"Hello?" she repeated. Her voice was more tentative now.

"Lauren, it's Richard."

"Gannon. I'm so glad you called," she said softly.

She sounded happy to hear from him, he thought. He leaned forward, resting his elbows on the desk, his chin on his knuckles. The receiver dangled loosely in his right hand. He looked at the shadow of himself on the screen of the computer terminal on his desk. "Lauren..." My darling. No! His fingers tightened on the cold plastic. He wanted to hit something, plunge his hand through the blank screen. He wouldn't admit even to himself that what he really wanted to do was cry.

"Did you find the boy?"

"No. It was a false lead."

"I'm sorry. I hope you find him soon."

"Yeah. Me, too." The leather chair creaked slightly under his weight. "Lauren, I can't make you any promises...."

"It's all right, Richard. I understand," she said evenly.

"But I'll be up this weekend if you still want me to come."

He heard that funny little catch in her breath. "Really?"

He smiled reluctantly. "Really," he responded.

LAUREN REPLACED THE RECEIVER and looked warily at her brother, standing in the open doorway of her bedroom. "He's coming on Friday," she said, unable to keep the smile of relief off her face.

Slade snorted and pivoted toward the hall. "You'd have gotten what you deserve if he'd told you to go to hell," he said over his shoulder. "Honestly, Lauren, I can't believe you did such a stupid thing."

Lauren followed him; they had been on their way to the stables when the phone rang. Slade had insisted on some exercise. He said he needed to stretch his muscles after the long flight, but she knew her brother. He thought the prescription for all ills was the sun on your face, the wind in your hair and a horse under you.

Maybe he was right; maybe she did need that prescription. She realized she looked awful. It didn't take her brother's horrified expression when he arrived to tell her that. Slade had always been the closest of her siblings. He knew her too well. Trying to avoid an explanation for the dark circles under her eyes and the tremor around her lips was as impossible as emptying the sea with a teaspoon.

The horses were ready for them, skittish and eager. Lauren hesitated. She wasn't the accomplished rider Slade was. But he wasn't about to let her back out. He chose the gentler mount and gave her a leg up. "Come on," he ordered as he mounted his horse and led the way out of the stableyard.

"Yes, sir," she grumbled.

A half-hour later she was grateful that she'd let her brother bully her into the ride. It had certainly blown the cobwebs out of her brain and put some of the color back in her cheeks.

They dismounted near the lake. Slade looped the reins of her horse and his over a branch of a shrub and sat down on the grass. He patted the patch beside him. "Have a seat."

She joined him, sitting cross-legged.

"Now, little sister, I am about to deliver a lecture. You can listen or not, but I have to say what I have to say."

"Just please don't tell me how stupid my scheme was. Believe me, I know."

"Lauren I realize that you're a grown woman, but in some ways you've been left in some kind of time warp. When it comes to men you're still the twenty-two-year-old you were with Monty."

She started to protest, but his next words stopped her. "I know Richard Gannon."

"You know—"

"Not personally," he corrected himself. "Some very good friends of mine had use of his company's services. They couldn't sing his praises loudly enough. But they also were of the opinion that he'd be the wrong man to cross."

"That's not so," Lauren denied. "Richard is strong, but he's fair. He's a wonderful person, Slade."

Slade gave her an enigmatic look. "Then he didn't deserve what you did to him, did he?" he asked softly.

Her head fell forward, her hair veiling her expression from him. "No," she said quietly.

"Lauren, you can describe your motives in any terms you like. You say you want a baby, a husband. What you really want is someone to fill the vacant places in your life. Don't try to fool yourself. You're lonely. I can understand that—so am I. We've both experienced the trauma of a bad engagement and neither of us is the type who can just dismiss it. Some people could, but to us an engagement is as good a committment as marriage. All I ask of you now is to be honest with yourself and Gannon. Don't marry for any reason other than love. And if things work out between the two of you, let yourself love him, wholeheartedly, with no reservations."

Lauren was quiet for a long time. She knew the effort the words had taken, the cost to her brother. In a way his experience had been worse than hers. His engagement had been to a woman he had known and trusted all his life. "Thanks, Slade. I don't know what will happen or how I'll react . . . but thanks."

He gave her a quick look, searching for sarcasm. But she was smiling gently. "I'd like to see you take your own advice someday, too. Let yourself love."

Slade made a noise in his throat. "Doubtful," he said.

5

RED WILDING WAS WAITING at the airport the following Friday evening when Richard arrived. "Hope you don't mind my meeting you, Gannon. Sarah has Lauren running errands for her."

"Not at all." Richard suspected the older man of contriving to have this interview, but he smiled pleasantly and climbed into the Jeep.

Red reached across the back seat and came up with two cans. He popped the tab on a beer and handed it to Richard. "Here. I always carry a cooler in the back seat." He opened a Coke for himself.

"Thanks." Richard loosened his tie and settled back. He took a swallow and sighed. "That's good." The past week had been a long one.

"I'll be glad when this foolishness is over. Parties!" he snorted. "Breakfast parties, lunch parties, dinner parties." He sighed. "If it weren't so damn hot in Florida I'd move the whole family to our place in Palm Beach for the month. Sarah likes parties, though...so do Marshall and his wife."

Richard grinned to himself at the thought of Marshall and Regina.

Red caught the grin and returned it. "Yeah. They love it all." He sobered, and his voice held a trace of sadness. "Marshall had to make a lot of changes in his life after my heart attack. He was the only one of my children who was interested in following in my footsteps, but neither of us had expected I would have to retire so early."

"How old was he when he took over for you?"

"Twenty-eight. It's been hard on him."

Richard didn't envy Marshall Wilding. Running the Wilding empire was a tremendous responsibility for such a young man. Richard was no stranger to the burdens that went along with responsibility, but, then, he didn't have to answer to a board of directors. Gannon Consultants and its three hundred and eighty-nine employees were under his direct control. "Marshall certainly has a good reputation in business," he said honestly.

The remark pleased Red. "He's done well. Regina has convinced him that being seen in all the right places is deadly important. She's a perfect corporate wife, but I sometimes wonder if he'd married someone else ... Oh, well." He shrugged. "Lauren, now, doesn't care too much for the social scene."

"Really?" Richard didn't know why he was surprised, except she was such an outgoing, gregarious creature. He tugged the tie free of his collar and shoved it into his pocket.

"She enjoys people," said Red, reading his mind. "But she's like me. She prefers to get together with small groups of good friends." He laughed heartily. "I don't know why I'm telling you. You must know all this."

"No, we've had less time than I would have liked to get to know the little things about each other." The response was evasive, but he didn't know how much Lauren had told her father about last weekend.

"She's been a little bit uptight this week. I suppose it's all the fuss about your engagement. Lauren was engaged once before, you know."

Richard settled more comfortably against the seat. It was obvious that he was about to gain some welcome insight into Lauren Wilding. "Yes, I knew she was engaged. But she's never told me much about the man."

"Fine family, but the fellow was a gold digger of the worst sort. Of course I had to let her sort it out for herself. Wouldn't do to come on as the heavy father."

Richard was certain Lauren would kill both of them if she knew they were discussing her this way, but he needed all the information he could gather if he planned to challenge her. "How did she find out?" he asked.

Red shot him an amused grin. "Well, you know how she feels about that business of hers?"

Richard nodded and took another swallow of the cold beer.

"Darned if she hasn't done a fine job," Red digressed proudly. "She's turned out to be quite a businesswoman."

Richard was itching to prod him about Lauren's other fiancé, but he held his tongue.

"Anyway, the fellow started making plans to join her in the business. It was just getting off the ground then. She kept quiet for a long time, I guess thinking that the two of them working together wouldn't be such a bad thing. But then he started giving advice, making decisions, talking about all the changes he was going to make in the way Tender Age was run."

Richard had to smile at the thought of any man so badly misjudging Lauren Wilding. "I can imagine how she reacted to that."

"Poor fellow wasn't perceptive enough to see her getting steamier and steamier." Red chuckled. "Finally one day she blew. Got a jaw like a bulldog, ya know. Stubborn and headstrong to match."

Richard thought Lauren's jaw was beautiful and delicate, but he didn't argue with her father about her being headstrong.

Red went on. "She faced him down, told him Tender Age was her baby and asked what he planned to contribute to the marriage."

"What did he answer to that?" Gannon lifted the can to his mouth.

"The stupid fellow said, 'Genes, of course, darling. You can't find better genes.'"

Red's high-pitched mimic and the idea of Lauren's reaction to the man's presumption set Richard off. He choked first on the beer and then on his laughter.

Red pounded him on the back until he regained his breath, then joined in with a lively chuckle. "I believe I like you, son. One other thing I'll tell you. I worried about her. She changed after the engagement was broken. She threw every bit of herself into that business, left no room for softer emotions. It just about broke my heart to see her that way. Since then everything's been business, only business."

Richard didn't comment, but to himself he thought that everything still was only business to Lauren Wilding.

They were approaching the house along the drive, when Red observed, "She's back."

The laughter, shared with the older man, had served to loosen some of the tension and ease the leaden, empty feeling inside Richard. He watched as Lauren came out of the garage. She seemed to hesitate for a brief second before she continued on a path that would put her at the front porch about the same time they pulled to a stop. She wore flat sandals and a blue sundress that just skimmed her knees. Richard noted that she must have spent some time in the sun this past week, because her shoulders were tanned to a honey gold. Lord, she looked beautiful. Richard felt his throat close.

Red had one more piece of information to impart. "Gannon, I hate people who give unsolicited advice, but I'm going to give some, anyway. Lauren's been kind of down in the dumps this week. I sense that something happened between the two of you last weekend."

Richard finished off his beer. The can became a mangled mass in his fist, but he maintained his silence.

Red eased off on the accelerator. "What I want to say is this. She's independent to a fault—headstrong and foolish about some things. But she's smart and loyal, and for a man who's strong enough, she'd be a whiz of a wife."

Richard stared out the window at Lauren. He didn't respond because he didn't know what to say.

"Damn it, boy! She's got spunk."

Finally Richard turned to him. "Spunk, hell! She's a rich, spoiled brat!"

He wouldn't have been surprised if Red had turned the Jeep around and taken him back to the airport immediately. He was surprised by the chuckle, then the laugh, that erupted from the older man.

"She is that, as well," conceded Red. "If you want another bit of advice . . ."

"I don't," said Richard shortly.

"You'll march right up those steps and flat plant one on her."

Richard looked at the older man through narrowed eyes. He shook his head and smiled in spite of himself. "I haven't heard that saying in years."

"It's a good saying," said Red under his breath. "Works, too."

LAUREN STEELED HERSELF when she heard the sound of the approaching Jeep. Since Richard's phone call on Wednesday her emotions had ricocheted from contrition to self-reproach to hope, with hope barely struggling for life. It had been the longest two days of her life.

Her guarded expression as she watched her father and Richard leap from the Jeep to the ground quickly changed to one of suspicion. She searched her father's innocent blue eyes, but found nothing there. She hoped he hadn't given Richard a lecture.

However, something about Richard was different. He looked wonderful, but as he came toward her his gaze raked her brazenly. He looked like a man who might be willing to buy if the price was right. He even walked differently. He'd always moved with the self-confidence of a successful man, but this was more of a swagger. She didn't like it at all.

She'd admit to having made a terrible mistake. She'd done something very wrong in trying to manipulate him. But if he thought he could just walk in here and . . .

She had no time for further thought. He snaked out an arm and drew her close. Her breath escaped on a little puff at the soft collision of their bodies.

Disregarding their audience, Richard moved his mouth hungrily over her lips, immediately warming her, scattering her judgment to the winds. She responded thankfully, sliding her hands under his jacket, around his back, grasping handfuls of his shirt

Win "Instantly" right now in another way
...try our Preview Service

Get 4 FREE full-length Harlequin Temptation books

Plus this handy, compact umbrella
(a $10.00 retail value alone)

Plus a surprise free gift

Plus lots more!

Our love stories are popular everywhere...and WE'RE CELEBRATING with free birthday prizes—free gifts—and a fabulous no-strings offer.

Simply try our Preview Service. With your trial, you get SNEAK PREVIEW RIGHTS to four new HARLEQUIN TEMPTATION novels a month—months before they are in stores—with 11%-OFF retail on any books you keep (just $1.99 each)—and Free Home Delivery besides.

THERE IS NO CATCH. You're not required to buy a single book, ever. You may even cancel Preview Service privileges anytime, if you want. The free gifts are yours anyway, as tokens of our appreciation.

It's a super sweet deal if ever there was one. Try us and see.

Harlequin Temptation™ Free Gifts–Free Prizes

86738

YES I'll try the Harlequin Preview Service under the terms specified herein. Send me 4 free books and all the other FREE GIFTS. I understand that I also automatically qualify for ALL "Super Celebration" prizes and prize features advertised in 1986. I have written my birthday below. Tell me on my birthday what I win.

WIN A GREAT PRIZE

142 CIX 2515

► If you are NOT signing up for Preview Service, DO NOT use seal. You can win anyway.

PLEASE PRINT

NAME

ADDRESS   APT #

CITY

STATE   ZIP

FILL IN BIRTHDAY INFORMATION BELOW

MONTH   DATE

This month's featured prizes—a dream come true MINK or FOX jacket, winner's choice + as an added bonus, a world renowned delight, Godiva Chocolates for 101 other winners.

PLEASE PICK FUR JACKET YOU WANT ☐ FOX ☐ MINK. Gift offer limited to new subscribers, one per household, and terms and prices subject to change.

Harlequin
"Super Celebration" Sweepstakes
901 Fuhrmann Blvd.
P.O. Box 1325
Buffalo, NY 14269

PLACE
1ST CLASS
STAMP
HERE

to hold herself upright. Even had her eyes not been closed she would have been blind to their surroundings, heedless of anything save the scent and strength and sensuality of the man who held her.

Finally he lifted his head.

At the loss of his lips she opened her eyes and let loose a whisper. "Don't . . ."

He frowned. The hands on her back slipped a fraction.

"Don't let go of me."

His smile of satisfaction would have been met with caution, had she been able to stand on her own, had she not been so thankful that he seemed to have forgiven her.

"Why shouldn't I let you go?"

Lauren realized he wasn't content with a suggestion of what he was doing to her; he wanted it spelled out. She could give him that, she decided; she felt stronger now. Her lips curved into a smile. "Because I'll fall. Your kisses are powerful stuff, Gannon."

"So are yours, Wilding."

Her eyes danced with pleasure; she laughed softly. "Are they?"

"Definitely." He stood her firmly on her feet but kept one hand at her waist. Only then did she realize that her parents were standing off to the side of the porch, watching with undisguised enjoyment.

Lauren cleared her throat. "Oh." She cleared it again and pasted a smile on her face. "Are you ready to leave?" she asked brightly.

Her mother's face fell. "Aren't you and Richard going with us to the Talbots' barbecue?"

"I don't think so, Mother."

"But Richard hasn't met Slade." Sarah turned to Richard. "Lauren's brother has gone on ahead."

"Leave the youngsters alone, Mother," put in Red. "He can meet Slade tomorrow. We're all going to breakfast at the track, aren't we?"

"Yes, that's right," Lauren concurred eagerly, wondering at the reversal of roles. Her mother seemed reluctant to leave them alone, while her father seemed to be promoting it.

Richard gave Sarah one of his most charming smiles. "I asked Lauren not to make any plans for this evening. We've barely had time to talk since I came home from Amsterdam. I hope you'll forgive me."

"Of course. I understand. But what about dinner? I've given the cook the night off and Shaw has gone to visit his sister."

Lauren opened her mouth again, only to have her position as spokesperson usurped once more.

"I'm sure we can find something."

If her father thought it strange that Lauren was allowing Richard to do her talking for her, he didn't comment. He simply said, "We'll take another car and leave the Jeep for you in case you want to use it." He took Sarah's arm and turned her firmly toward the garage.

It was the perfect distraction. "Of course we'll take another car. If you thought I was going to arrive at the Talbots' in that thing, Will Wilding, you're . . ."

Lauren watched them go. Now that she and Richard were alone she wasn't sure how to broach the subject that had been left hanging last weekend. "Well . . ." she hedged, tucking her hair behind her ear. "I guess we could take your suitcase upstairs."

"That's a good idea," said Richard blandly. He went back to the Jeep and reached in for the tan leather bag. They entered the house and climbed the staircase in silence. He followed her to the same room he'd occupied the week before. Lauren opened the door and stood aside for him to enter. Instead of crossing the threshold, he dropped the bag inside the room and paused, turning toward her.

"Don't you think we ought to lay a few ground rules?"

"Yes, we should," Lauren agreed. Her gaze slipped to the dresser, where the ring winked at her again. "You left something last time." She nodded toward it.

"I know."

Well, she had her answer, and it was just about what she feared it would be. "Did you leave it there to punish me?"

He looked truly surprised. "No. I had no intention of punishing you, Lauren. The ring just didn't seem to mean much anymore."

She gave an exasperated sigh and put her hands on her hips, facing him squarely. "Well, do something with it. I don't want to have to keep hiding the thing from the maids."

Richard wandered over to the dresser. He stood looking down at the ring for a minute before picking it up and dropping it into his pocket. He returned to the threshold to face her. Sliding his hands into his pockets, he leaned against the doorjamb and crossed his ankles. "Does that mean you don't like it?"

"It's beautiful." She crossed her arms across her chest and fitted her spine to the door facing. They were only inches away from each other, but the inches might have been miles. Her voice became very soft. "I didn't mean to snap at you. It's been a long week."

"For me, too," he said, watching her levelly. "What do you think we should do about this situation?"

She looked directly into his eyes. "You know what I want, Richard," she said without faltering. "I still feel that we have the basis for a wonderful marriage. The question is, what do you want to do?"

Richard examined the toes of his brown leather loafers. "Well," he said slowly, meditatively. "I've done a lot of thinking this week. One good thing has come out of the whole mess."

She maintained a calm expression, but it didn't matter. He wasn't looking at her; he spoke to his shoes. "I've been able to put my feelings for you into a kind of rational perspective. I think I loved you too much. It wasn't healthy."

Lauren clenched her jaw.

Finally he lifted his gaze. "I had you up on a pretty high pedestal."

She searched his gray eyes, but they revealed nothing. "I never wanted to be on a pedestal," she protested.

"I know. I put you there, anyway. It was my mistake."

"And now?"

"Now...." He dragged the word out, meditated for a long moment that seemed to stretch to infinity. Lauren felt a powerful urge to scream.

"Now there is one very important thing you've ignored in your deliberations—the physical aspect of marriage. We've never—" Richard deliberately avoided the words *made love* "—had sex. I think we should try it out. If we're good in bed..." He shrugged.

Lauren swallowed, trying to keep the shock she felt at the hard words from her expression. "It sounds rather unemotional and cold-blooded," she evaded.

"You didn't want emotion, remember?" His eyes shot silver flames, and he dropped his voice. "Besides, I don't feel cold-blooded at all. Quite the contrary."

She held his gaze, even though her heart had accelerated dramatically at his words. "And if we find that we're compatible?"

He shrugged again. "We can reassess our options."

Lauren tried to tell herself she wasn't disappointed at his pragmatic, businesslike attitude. It was very much the same as her own had been when she'd first begun to think about marriage.

"Well?"

The one word, uttered shortly, brought her back to the present. When she might have been glad to see anger in his eyes, she saw only guarded amusement. "I think you're playing with me," she said quietly.

Unexpectedly the veil fell from his expression. In the brief glimpse, before he could resurrect the indifference, she saw the bleakness that had haunted him all week. "Not exactly playing. This isn't a subject for frivolity. The truth of the matter is, Lauren, I haven't known what to do."

It was quite an admission from a man as strong and decisive as Richard Gannon, but the truth was more than that. The truth was in his admission that he'd loved her too much. She recognized that his feeling for her was damaged, possibly destroyed, and the loss was more painful than she could ever have imagined.

She let her head fall back to rest on the wood. "As I see it we have three choices. One, we could go on with the engagement story for now, but you could go back to Philadelphia. No one else knows that we planned a wedding at the end of the month. After Labor Day we can announce that it just didn't work out. Two, we can start over, get to know each other as we should have in the first place. Or three, we can just call the whole thing off, immediately and completely."

She felt the thrill of hope reborn when she saw the denial in his eyes even before he spoke. Levering himself forward, he rested his arm on the jamb above her head. The proximity of his hard body sent a river of warmth through her. She had to caution herself not to wrap her arms around him, not to seek the embrace she'd once thought of as a haven.

"No. I'm not ready to call it off completely. Which eliminates numbers one and three," he said decisively. "And you left out my choice."

She raised her eyes to his.

"We can try out the physical side of this relationship. If we're good in bed, I'll put that ring on your finger and we can go on with our plans just as though nothing had happened."

Lauren's every instinct revolted at his callous suggestion. Half of her wanted to refuse outright, but the other half urged caution. She had known a travesty of love at twenty-two, and desire since then. But sex itself had never quite lived up to its promise. "Is that enough of a basis for marriage?"

He gave a short laugh. "It's as much as you had when you began to plan this whole thing." A finger touched her shoulder, traced slowly over the bare skin to her neck. His voice was husky with the beginnings of desire. "You had certain standards that had to be met by a prospective husband. I have one or two myself."

His lazy touch, the scent of him, stirred hungry responses in her, until suddenly she couldn't bear his nearness. She ducked under his arm and crossed the hall to sink gratefully onto the sofa.

Richard followed more slowly. He lowered himself to sit beside her. Leaning forward, he took a peach from the bowl of fruit on the coffee table. He seemed content to wait—not impatiently, either.

Lord, what a mess she'd made of everything. "All right, Gannon. I'll agree to your suggestion." She turned her head to look at him. "But I won't wear the ring. Not yet." Her eyes fell under the quick displeasure in his. "I-I mean, I can't."

"Deception isn't a standard part of your makeup, is it, Lauren," he asked somberly.

"Believe it or not, it isn't." She met his gaze straight on, seeking understanding in his eyes but finding only mild curiosity. "I will be honest with you from now on, Richard. I promise."

"At least that's something." For a moment he held the fruit in his big hand, one finger stroking over its downy surface just as it had stroked her neck. She could almost feel the heat from memory. Then his strong white teeth bit through the soft skin to the tender flesh inside.

Lauren watched, fascinated, as a droplet of juice lingered on his bottom lip, threatening to run down his chin. He caught it with his tongue as he inhaled the scent the fruit had released. "Umm. Sweet and juicy. Delicious," he said.

She would never have believed such simple words could be so erotic, but they were, especially when delivered in a voice grown husky and suggestive.

Suddenly she realized that he was doing this deliberately, enjoying the fruit with every sense, sending a message that he intended to enjoy her, too, tonight.

He stretched his arm across the space separating them, holding the peach an inch from her lips. "Want a bite?"

Lauren's throat felt so dry that she automatically opened her mouth. The sweetness was balanced with just the right amount of tang to stimulate the juices in her mouth. It was delicious. She licked her lips. His dark, smoke-colored eyes followed the motion, and she realized she had done just what he'd expected. She felt a shiver race along her spine despite the warmth of the evening.

This was ridiculous. She had to get hold of herself. "I think a swim would be nice. What about you?" she asked in a rush, then cursed herself for being so obvious.

Leaning forward, he presented her with a view of his broad back. He disposed of the half-eaten fruit in an ashtray and dug into his pocket with his other hand. She watched the muscles move under the white cotton shirt. Very deliberately he wiped his fingers with his handkerchief before he answered, "That depends."

She blinked. "Depends on what?"

Looking back over his shoulder, he smiled knowingly. "Would a swim relax you? You're as tense as a bow string."

"That's crazy," she protested. "I don't need relaxing."

He went on as though she hadn't spoken. "I doubt you're a virgin," he mused. "But for some reason you're acting like one. The only excuse that comes to mind is that you've never particularly enjoyed sex."

She stood abruptly, angered by his perception but determined he shouldn't know how right he was. "Look, Gannon. I'm not a virgin and I'm not tense. If I'm nervous it's because you're acting like a cocky chauvinist. So why don't we just get this over with?"

Richard studied the pulse that throbbed in her throat, the clenched fists at her sides, the stiffness in her shoulders, and felt sympathy welling up within him. Acting like a cocky chauvinist was his only protection right now. He hadn't meant to scare her, though, and she was scared as hell. The Wilding self-confidence was not only wavering; it was non-existent. Strangely, the thought didn't give him any satisfaction.

He wasn't sure of his feelings for her. The bitterness was still there—a resentment that wouldn't be forgotten quickly. However, it had been temporarily displaced with a protective tenderness he couldn't explain and was damn sure he didn't want to feel.

Slowly he got to his feet and circled the table. He wanted her more than any other woman he had ever known, but he didn't want her scared. He wanted her wide awake and fully participating, and he intended to have her that way or not at all. He lifted her hand, holding her wrist while he gently pried her fingers open.

Raising her hand to his lips, he placed a sensual kiss in her palm. "Get it over with? Lauren, a sexual experience between a man and a woman should be something beautiful, mutually desired. I want to make love to you. You must know how much I want that. But you have to want it, too."

The lips at her palm were hot against her skin, lighting leaping, hungry flames in her belly. *Make love?* Before he had said *have sex*.

Lauren had fought the threat of emotional involvement all week long, was still fighting it. This was what frightened her, not the physical aspect. She'd tried to tell herself that the reason she was so upset was because everything she'd worked and planned for was down the drain. But that was a lie. And now, she thought disgustedly, all he had to do was change the wording of the request and she was not only willing, she was eager to melt into his arms.

Well, she would agree to his terms, but she would keep her guard up. She didn't hesitate any longer. "We could swim later," she said huskily. The eyes that blazed back at his were resolute. Slowly she raised her arms to lock them around his neck.

"Later," Richard agreed, gratified by the smile that was half sweet and half sexy as hell. He lowered his head. The taste of peach was still on her lips, mingling sensually with the taste of her. When she re-

sponded, tightening her arms, his heart accelerated to
a primitive beat and he hauled her against him.

Primitive—that was how this woman suddenly
made him feel by her boldness—primitive and uncivilized. In a quick move calculated to dominate, Richard backed her against the wall. But the ploy didn't
work. The minute he felt her warm and pliant against
him, he lost his sense of reality.

He raised his head, drew air into his lungs. "Damn
you, Wilding!" he groaned, and then his mouth came
down in a reckless, savage kiss. She met the kiss with
no hesitation at all, her mouth opening under the on-
slaught of his probing tongue.

He pulled her away from the wall and melded her
against him. His fingers sought the zipper at her back,
lowered it with a quick rasp and swept the straps forward. Before the dress had time to reach the floor, his
hands were on her breasts and hers were tearing at the
buttons of the shirt he wore. Even had she been
thinking straight, she wouldn't have been able to explain this wild and fundamental desire, this overwhelming eroticism that engulfed her, like another
person inhabiting her body.

She inhaled sharply at the sensation of heat from
his palms. The crumpled dress settled around her ankles. She kicked it aside. Her hands roamed over the
musculature of his chest, her nails scraping lightly.

He squeezed her breasts, felt the response as her
nipples hardened, and then his hands were all over

her, moving restlessly, around her midriff, up her back to her shoulders, down her spine to her hips.

When he lifted her hard against him, she shifted, her sensitive breasts aching for the abrasion of his hair-roughened chest. He groaned harshly and his tongue plunged deeper, ravishing the tender flesh inside her mouth.

Lauren didn't know how they got to the bed. Whether he carried her or she walked, she had no idea, but they were there. He pushed her down until she was sitting on the edge of the mattress. The hunger in his eyes as they raked her almost naked body touched off answering flames, heating her blood, sending it steaming through her veins. She fell back on one elbow while he knelt before her to remove her sandals.

His hands massaged her calves, then slid slowly, deliberately up her thighs, under the lace that edged her bikini panties. His fingers rested lightly on her hipbones, thumbs brushing her stomach, provoking a muscular contraction. Her eyes fell shut on pinwheels of light as she inhaled a cry. Her head dropped back. "Gannon . . ."

Then his fingers were tracing an erotic half circle to meet in the warm, moist softness between her legs. He made a muffled, satisfied sound from deep in his throat and rose to his feet, like some large predator looming over her. She lifted her head again, opening her eyes to the mesmerizing fire in his.

The sides of his shirt hung open. Lauren could see the slick sheen of perspiration on his neck, his chest. He was so beautiful, she thought, so very beautiful. Though his eyes glittered dangerously, they held an intensity of desire in their smoky, mysterious depths that she'd never seen before, and it touched off a responsive yearning in her that she'd never felt before.

One large hand rested on her stomach; with the other he stripped the lace scrap from her and tossed it away. He wasn't gentle and she didn't want gentleness. She arched against the weight, instinctively seeking more of the animal pleasure he was offering.

Suddenly, without warning, his silver gaze came up to lock with hers. The impact was heart stopping.

Richard looked down at Lauren, and all his doubts and mistrust faded away. Those feelings had no place in the present. They were irrelevant to this moment. Perhaps they would return, but for now he was relieved to see them go. For now his sole intent was to release the passion in this exquisite woman, expose the vulnerability she'd hidden under the guise of pragmatic businesswoman.

He'd once thought he didn't care for clinging vines. But now he was surprised to find that he wanted her to cling, to go crazy with her need for him. Him and only him.

Her gaze met his in a breathless visual duel in which she could read his absolute refusal to abandon supremacy in this moment. And finally she surrendered the moment to him. As she collapsed on the mattress, he knelt again, and she felt his warm breath on her skin, nibbling, tasting, whispering unintelligible words, until, after an interminable time, she stretched upward into the vortex of a spinning black world. She was insane with need.

His hands slid under her hips and held her to him. He drove her to peak after peak. Her breathing was coming in raw, hungry gasps; her body was aflame with life and energy. And light—a strange, brilliance behind her lids illuminated the universe with a pyrotechnical display. She thought it would never end, that she wouldn't survive the seemingly endless jolts of electrical shock, but at last they began to fade in the darkness.

Weakly she opened her eyes, turned her head against the sheet to watch him through her lashes. He was tearing at his clothes with feverish haste. And in a moment his big body was covering hers, his hips pushing her deep into the mattress, his chest hot and damp against her tender skin. She began to speak, but her words were lost forever as he entered her, hard and strong, swollen with desire.

She found that her hunger was unappeased. His mouth sought hers, taking large mock bites before fusing over her lips. Her nails dug into his shoulders, and she heard a small growl of response as he thrust deeper and deeper, filling her completely, demanding that she take all of him. They climbed together this time, and the fireworks were larger, brighter, exploding outward and inward until every nerve, every muscle, every atom of her body was burned by their fire.

The shudders continued rippling through Lauren's body even after Richard had rolled aside with a hoarse moan and wrapped her in his arms.

"Oh, Gannon," she whispered, still dazed and disoriented, minutes, hours, aeons later. "What did you do to my inhibitions?"

He chuckled, the sound low and lusty against her neck. "Blew them to hell and back, I hope. I have no use for inhibitions in my bed."

"I noticed." She stretched luxuriously and drew away far enough to see him. His hair was rumpled. She vaguely remembered plunging her fingers through its thickness. "It was different from what I expected."

His mouth twisted wryly. "You mean because I didn't play the gentleman to your lady in bed?"

"That isn't exactly what I meant." Her brows came together in a small frown. "I don't think."

Richard eyed her oddly for a minute, then rolled away from her to get to his feet. He crossed the room to where his jacket lay across his suitcase and returned with a package of cigarettes and a lighter.

Lauren pulled the sheet up over her. "I didn't know you smoked," she said as he joined her under the sheet.

Leaning against the headboard, he gathered her under one arm and held a lighter to the cigarette. "I smoke occasionally," he said. He inhaled deeply and sent the smoke toward the ceiling on a sigh.

Lauren chewed at her lower lip for a minute. This wasn't going to be easy. "Can I ask you something?"

"Of course," he answered quietly.

Cuddling closer, she half buried her face in his chest. "I guess what I really want to do is tell you that you were right. About the sex, I mean."

Richard didn't answer.

"It was more wonderful than I'd ever imagined," she whispered, her cheeks warm. He was unnaturally still. She risked a peek at his face. He was staring down at her with a strange expression on his face. She tried, and failed, to read more than simple interest there.

Her blue eyes sparked with irritation. "I suppose to you it was just sex," she snapped.

Richard wanted to deny it. He wanted to tell her that what they'd just shared was the most glorious experience of his life. He wanted to say that she was the only woman he'd ever feel such passion for. He wanted to say, "I love you, I adore you."

But he savagely bit back the impulse. No more undying declarations of love. Not from him. Not until he heard some from her. He forced himself to maintain a facade of geniality. Grinning outrageously, he said, "It was very nice." At her reaction, he almost choked on his laughter.

She sat up, her spine as straight as a ramrod. "Nice? *Nice*? Well, thank you very much! What would you like to do next? I hope I can keep you as nicely entertained for the rest of the evening."

He hid his grin. "I'm sure you can. Suppose we start by raiding your mother's refrigerator."

The turnaround stunned her. She gaped at him. "Now? But I thought . . ."

"That we would stay in bed until morning?" He laughed in genuine amusement and pulled her up beside him. She calmed a bit in his arms as his laughter tickled her neck. "I don't intend to be totally uncivilized. Besides, I'm starving. I haven't eaten since breakfast."

"Except for that damn peach."

"Except for the peach," he agreed blandly.

6

THEY WORKED IN SILENCE. Lauren placed a jar of kosher dills and a bag of potato chips on a tray along with a platter of turkey sandwiches. Richard was being annoyingly smug about her ecstatic response to his lovemaking.

She supposed he had cause. Her passion had left her shaken, unsure of her ability to cope with such strong feelings. She almost laughed aloud at the memory of her determination to avoid a deep emotional involvement.

Richard carried the tray out to the terrace. After taking two bottles of beer from the refrigerator, Lauren grabbed a handful of napkins and an opener and followed him. Walking behind him, she took the opportunity to study his magnificent body. He was now dressed in jeans and a knit polo shirt, and his shoulders looked very broad, his hips very lean.

They ate in silence, too. Lauren's nerves grew more and more taut as the August sun dipped to sit lightly on the crest of a hill, and her senses were somehow intensely keen. The blazing orb seemed more golden, the scent of roses from her mother's garden headier, the songs of the birds sweeter than she had ever noticed them being.

She wasn't sure how to react to Richard's rather offhand attitude toward their lovemaking. Their roles had seemingly been reversed. She was the one who couldn't keep her fascination under control. Trying very hard not to look at his mouth, she took apart a sandwich and ate a sliver of turkey. Out of the corner of her eye she saw his hands wrapped around a sandwich.

Those long, talented fingers had brought her so much more than mere physical delight; she could almost feel the sensation of them gliding over her skin. But she also remembered the caring demand in their touch—the demand that she respond freely, fervidly, holding nothing back.

She munched a potato chip. When she looked again, the knoll had sliced a triangle out of the sun.

Meanwhile, Richard was devoting himself to the impromptu picnic with gusto. He finished three sandwiches, a huge handful of chips and his beer.

Damn him. He was so nonchalant, while her nerves were stretched to the breaking point. "Would you like my beer?" she asked.

"No, thanks. This is enough." He glanced over. "You're not eating."

How in the world could he think of food at a time like this? Her world had spun off its axis and he wanted to eat. "I ate some. I'm not very hungry."

"Then why don't we take the swim you suggested earlier."

Swim? Her body had grown so lethargic she would probably sink. "Feel free. I'm not in the mood myself."

Richard stifled a grin. "What are you in the mood for, then?"

Her eyes flew to his face, giving her away.

He chuckled, then rose, stretched and patted his flat stomach. "Oh, we'll get back to that, too." He reached for her hand and drew her up into the circle of his arms. She couldn't resist hooking her hands over his shoulders. He brought her closer and she sighed as she settled against him.

"A swimming pool presents all sorts of possibilities for making love, you know," he murmured into her hair. His hand stroked up and down her back in a soothing touch.

"Does it?" she said huskily. Her cheek rested on his soft knit shirt. She linked her fingers behind his neck. He smelled so good.

His hands roamed over her rounded bottom. "C'mon, I'll show you."

SOFT CHIMES RANG delicately five times, then stopped. Lauren peeked through heavy lashes at the china clock, which was as dainty as its sound. The hands, fashioned of tiny gold leaves, pointed to five o'clock. She frowned, forgetting momentarily why she had set the alarm, since they'd had only three hours' sleep.

Then she remembered—they were going with her parents to breakfast at the track. But there was plenty of time yet. She snuggled against Richard's warm, hard body and closed her eyes again.

An hour later they were still fast asleep, when a hammerlike fist hit the door. "Up, brat!"

Lauren jerked upright at the racket.

Richard sat up, too, and looked around him, disoriented. "What the hell . . . ?"

Lauren flopped back on her pillow with a groan. "Okay!" she yelled.

Richard fell back, too. He breathed once, twice. They both lay there, staring at the ceiling. "What was that?" he finally asked.

"That was my brother Slade and his version of an alarm clock." Richard had to squint to see the clock in the early morning light. "It's only six."

"I told you we were going to breakfast at the track."

"Breakfast, yes."

She still stared up, reluctant to move. "We have to be there at six forty-five."

Richard rubbed a hand over his face. "I guess I thought a breakfast would be at some civilized time, say, eight o'clock." He yawned. "Or nine. Or even ten. After all, it's the weekend."

Lauren made a superhuman effort and sat up again. Whipping the covers aside she got to her feet, crossed to the closet and took out a robe. "If we wait until eight o'clock we won't find a seat."

Linking his hands behind his head, Richard watched her tie a white silk wrap around her narrow waist. "This isn't a small group, then?"

She lifted her hair from under the collar and grinned. "Between twelve and fourteen hundred. Do you have a quarter, Gannon?"

He lifted a dark brow. "Not on me. Why?"

"I was going to toss you for the shower, but I guess you lose by default."

He was on his feet before she could close the door behind her. "We'll share," he informed her, lifting her off her feet with an arm circling her waist. "Okay?"

She wound her arms around his neck and smiled sleepily. "Okay," she murmured. "Will we be late?"

"Count on it."

THE SARATOGA SUNRISE BREAKFAST at the race course had been a ritual for more than a century. The setting was splendid. Visitors could enjoy a sumptuous meal on the flower-bordered terrace while watching the thoroughbreds exercise in the morning mist.

Richard walked behind Lauren as she wove her way through the elegant crowd toward the table where her parents sat. Entranced by the back view, he let his gaze wander over her. Fluid sapphire silk shifted across her derriere and swung against her legs. She smiled at people in passing, her fine profile flirting from beneath a wide-brimmed straw hat banded in the same color of blue as her dress. The epitome of ladylike grace as she moved, she was at the same time a totally desirable woman. He'd been right about the passion that lay beneath her very proper facade.

He frowned, remembering the first of the countless times they'd made love through the night. She'd stimulated feelings in him that he'd been unaware of, a deep hunger that swept away on a tidal wave of sensuality the restraint he'd promised himself. They had made love again in the pool. With the edge of his desire slightly blunted, he'd thought he could hold himself in check. It didn't work out that way. Her responses were so sweet, so obviously unseasoned but eager, that it thrilled him to know he'd given her something no one else had.

His thoughts were interrupted when, through a loudspeaker over their heads, an announcer identified the horses as they passed. The name Wilding caught Richard's attention. Glad of a diversion, he shifted his gaze to the track spread out below them. He sought and found a spirited bay.

He was a beautiful animal—his proud neck high, his powerful flanks sleek and gleaming in the fall of morning light. He was led by a groom wearing what were obviously the Wilding colors: a red square in a white one bordered by blue. Richard recognized the international signal code for the letter W.

The exercise rider nudged the horse, and the animal stretched his trot into a slow gallop. Even among the other thoroughbreds Richard thought he was an exceptional horse.

"Gorgeous, isn't he?" Lauren had stopped walking and now smiled up at him. "His name is Last Bid."

"He's a magnificent animal," murmured Richard, not wanting to look away even though he realized they had reached the table.

"Meet his owner," Lauren offered.

A tall, lean man rose from the table to give her a kiss on the cheek.

"Richard, this is my brother Slade. I should caution you that if you show the least bit of interest he'll haul you off to the paddocks after breakfast. Slade, this is Richard Gannon."

Slade's handshake was firm, his smile indulgent when it was directed toward his sister and genial when he turned to Richard. His eyes were the same dark blue as Lauren's, but his hair was darker—a walnut color streaked by the sun. Richard found it easy to respond to the man's friendly regard.

"How are you, Gannon? Good to meet you." He put an affectionate arm around his sister. "I understand you've taken on the job of taming this filly. Let me warn you, it won't be easy."

Lauren held her breath—Slade knew very well what the situation was—but Richard only laughed, making no comment about the validity of the engagement. "Thanks for the warning."

At that moment, Sarah broke in. "Lauren, take Richard to the buffet. Be sure to have him try the Saratoga Hand melon."

He went with her to the serving line, a casual hand at her waist. Her gaze flicked to his. "Thanks," she said, handing him a warm plate and taking one for herself.

Richard didn't pretend to misunderstand. He shrugged and studied the fare spread out in the elegant buffet. "This looks good," he said, surveying the dishes. "What is the Saratoga Hand melon your mother was talking about?"

She indicated the bowls containing half a fruit, scooped out and filled with fresh strawberries, glistening and dewy in the morning light. "It's a cantaloupe lover's heaven. The pancakes are wonderful, too."

When they returned to the table, their plates were laden.

Richard had barely unfolded his napkin when Slade commented, "You were in Lexington last March. I heard about the work you did for the McClintocks."

An arched brow indicated Richard's surprise. Most of his clients were content to keep their business quiet, but the two young McClintocks who had inherited an outdated department store chain were obviously an exception. "They're nice people," he said noncommittally. He didn't know how much they'd told Slade about the financial disaster from which he'd helped them recover.

"Curt McClintock says you saved them from certain bankruptcy." Slade grinned. "Charlotte says quite a bit more than that."

Lauren shot Richard a glance. He grinned that sort of gratified grin she'd seen before. Was this Charlotte another old friend? He must have more ex-girls than a hound dog has fleas, she thought, unaware that her brows were knit in a cross frown.

A white-jacketed waiter poured coffee. "Would you like something else to drink?" he asked.

"I'll have another milk punch," Red told the man. He grinned at Richard. "Learned to drink these things down at Slade's place in Kentucky. They may not know much about breeding horses, but they mix a good drink."

There followed the same good-natured wrangle about New York-bred horses versus Kentucky-bred horses that Lauren and her mother had heard a hundred times.

"Slade!" "Daddy!" they protested at the same time.

"Sorry," Red apologized.

"I've never been around horses," Richard put in.

Sarah groaned; Lauren laughed.

Her brother loved an audience for his favorite topic. Richard asked a few pointed questions and was immediately included in the discussion of horses, leaving Lauren free to observe the way he fit in so smoothly. He might have always been a part of their family. She wasn't really very hungry, and after only a few bites she put down her fork. She reached for her coffee cup with one hand and lay the other on the white linen cloth.

Without a break in the conversation, Richard casually covered her fingers with his. She was startled but didn't move, enjoying the warmth. His hand only abandoned hers when he drank from his cup. Then it returned. The hand at her waist as they went through the buffet line had been more than a polite touch, too. Before today he'd never displayed casual affectionate gestures, but now he did it as easily as if they were in the habit of touching at every opportunity.

She was surprised to find that she liked it very much. She was surprised about a lot of things with Richard, not the least of which was how very exciting she found his lovemaking. He'd been right about the pool's presenting opportunities, she thought with a shimmer of wonderfully erotic memories.

Carefully she turned her hand over to meet his, palm to palm. His fingers immediately laced with hers. She smiled, contented.

Slade was saying something about the yearling sales that would be held next week, when she came back down to earth. "Oh, Slade. You're not going to try to outbid the Maktoum brothers, are you?"

"Maktoum brothers?" asked Richard. "The sheikhs from Dubai?"

Slade nodded wryly. "Would you believe they spent over fifty million one year at the Keeneland sales in Kentucky? Sheikh Bin Rashid al-Maktoum paid 10.2 million for one untried, unproved, year-old colt."

"By Northern Dancer out of My Bumpers. I'd say that was a good gamble," inserted Red.

"And how much did you pay for the colt's half brother, Slade?" Sarah asked sweetly.

"Considerably less than that, Mother. And it was the syndicate that bought the horse, not I." He grinned, explaining to Richard, "I started in the business eight years ago when a small operation came on the market, and I'm still the new kid on the block. Wildwood Farms is doing well, but it'll be a few years and a lot of luck before I can afford to pay that much for one horse."

Richard sat back in his chair, bringing their entwined hands to his thigh. "I'd like to see the paddock with you, Slade." Not familiar with the protocol, he hesitated before adding, "Can anyone attend the sales?"

Her father and Slade laughed, and Lauren groaned theatrically. Richard looked from one to the other in confusion until Sarah explained.

"Dealing with horseflesh is a heady, intoxicating passion, Richard...and addictive. Will has dabbled, but never plunged in, thank goodness. For the people who have, like Slade here, they eat, sleep and talk nothing but horses."

Richard smiled slowly. "Maybe I'll just dabble."

"Come along, then, Richard." Slade stood up. "While you're dabbling I'll pick your brain for some financial advice."

Richard stood, too, bringing Lauren up with him by the hand he still held. "You don't mind, do you?"

"Of course not. I love to watch the action in the backstretch. I might even talk to the horses and find myself a sure thing at the races this afternoon."

"If it's a sure thing you want, you'll put your money on Last Bid," advised her brother.

When they entered the paddock area Richard inhaled the earthy scent, mingled with another smell with which he was intimately familiar—the unmistakable smell of money. The whole area was reminiscent of a movie set he'd once seen. The high-priced horses were nursed and nurtured in the finest facilities by the most tender hands. Farriers, grooms, exercise boys and girls and trainers all carried out their work with earnest attention. The roan-colored turf was streaked with vivid silks and glistening coats. He felt his excitement growing.

In the pursuit of success Richard had seldom taken time out to simply amuse himself. Occasionally when he'd finished a job abroad he'd stay an extra day to see something of the country other than a boardroom. His one hobby, if it could be called a hobby, was the assimilation of knowledge. He liked to learn, and here was a fascinating new world to learn about.

Lauren watched the arrested expression on Richard's face. He was like a child who had discovered Christmas. She glanced up at Slade. His smile told her he'd recognized the signs, too.

Two hours later they were waiting near Last Bid's stall while Slade talked to the horse's trainer. "It's all very interesting, isn't it?" When she got no answer she laughed aloud.

"What?" Richard looked blankly at her for a minute, then grinned and pulled her close for a hug.

Yet another spontaneous sign of affection warmed her through and through. "I'm glad you're fond of my brother and his horses."

"Fond of them? The whole business is as captivating as your mother warned me it would be. I'd really like to know more."

Considering that Slade had been talking nonstop for two hours, Lauren thought Richard had probably learned a lot already. "There are some books at home I'm sure Slade would be happy to let you borrow."

Richard gave her a questioning look. "Are you feeling neglected?"

"Not at all," she assured him sincerely. "I'm very glad you're getting along with Slade so well. He and I have always been close."

For a moment Richard was caught in her smile, unable to pull his eyes away. The horses faded into oblivion. Suddenly he knew what he wanted. He wanted her again and forever. On any terms, he wanted her. And he didn't like the feeling one damn bit. It was much too soon to make such a decision, he told himself.

He forced his attention to Slade's discourse for the remainder of the tour, but his mind was more on the woman beside him. He reminded himself that she had deceived him, beguiled a marriage proposal out of him, pretended to be in love, when all she really wanted was a suitable husband and father for her child. If there ever was a child it would be his, as well, but she didn't seem to have thought of that.

"I'll leave you here," said Slade when they reached the gate. "If you're serious about attending the sales, Gannon, I'll see what I can do."

Richard shook Slade's hand. "I'd appreciate it."

"I'll see you two later."

"Are you really thinking about buying into a horse?" Lauren asked when they had left her brother.

"I might be."

"It's a big gamble."

"As you probably know, I can afford an occasional gamble. Didn't you run a D and B on me?" He was ashamed of the accusation as soon as the words left his mouth, but he had to have some security against this strong hunger.

Lauren felt the heat rise in her face. "That was a low blow, Gannon. Of course I didn't."

He looked disgusted with himself. "It was a low blow," he admitted. "Sorry. Come on, let's go." He turned and pulled her along after him as he made his way through the crowd.

"Where are we going?" Lauren asked when she'd recovered from the sudden change of direction.

He stopped, and she plowed into the back of him. "Somewhere to talk. You tell me where."

Shrugging, she pointed. Soon they were out on the street. She had to run to keep up with his long-legged stride. She tried to hold her hat in place with a palm on top of her head, but finally she gave up. Richard neatly avoided the pedestrians headed in the opposite direction. A few blocks farther they reached a small coffee house.

By the time they were seated, Lauren was winded and curious. "I thought you were interested in the horses," she said, placing her hat on the table.

"I am."

"Then why did you suddenly act as if you couldn't wait to get out of there?"

Richard took a deep breath and let it out slowly. "Because I had more important things on my mind."

He felt her withdraw from him, could almost see the protective wall she threw up. "Oh?" she said. "Have you come to a decision about us?"

A waiter stopped at their table. "Can I get you folks something? The menu's on the blackboard." He indicated the wall over their heads. "Our special for today is—"

"Two coffees," Richard interrupted. When the young man moved away to fill the order, he answered her question. "No, I haven't come to a decision, but I have been thinking about something you said."

There was a puzzled look on Lauren's face. "Something I said?"

He nodded. "When you were naming our options. You said we could get to know each other the way we should have in the first place." He reached across the table for her hand. "It's going to be damned hard now."

The gesture was one of affection, but Richard knew his features reflected his frustration. He'd thought he wanted her to surrender physically, that once they'd made love his confusion would begin to clear, he'd be able to think more objectively. It hadn't worked that way.

The waiter returned with their coffee. Lauren watched silently as he placed the steaming mugs on the table. "Why?" she asked.

"Because we've made love."

"I thought that was what you wanted."

"Hell, Lauren, you aren't stupid. Every time I touch you—it doesn't matter if we're in a crowd of people— I want to strip off that veneer of sophistication the way I did last night and make you wild with pleasure. Don't try to deny it. You did go crazy in my arms."

"I wouldn't dream of denying it." Her voice was unsteady. She paused, shooting him a glance. "You don't like that feeling?" she demanded, shaken by the picture his words evoked. She'd never known physical desire could be so devastating; nor had she allowed any man such power over her. In spite of all that, though, she felt the same way—a look, a touch, and she was on fire for him.

He studied their entwined fingers for a moment. His lips curved into a half smile. "I didn't say that. What I do feel is that while you respond beautifully when we're making love, at all other times there's a part of you that you hold in reserve. I'd like to get to know that part, as well."

Tell me you love me, Lauren. Tell me. I just may delude myself into believing it.

She dropped her gaze. "I . . . it isn't easy for me."

Richard sighed. "Quit blaming something that happened years ago between a child-woman and an arrogant young man," he said harshly. "The truth is you're afraid to let yourself open up. You're afraid of complete emotional involvement. And I'm not sure I'm willing to settle for anything less."

Lauren didn't bother to deny his accusation. He was right again, she thought sadly. Something in her makeup kept that last remnant of reserve intact.

"If anyone should be afraid of involvement it should be me."

At his statement she lifted her eyes to his. "I can't imagine your being afraid of anything," she murmured.

He drew his hand back to his side of the table and lifted the coffee mug to his lips. "How much do you know about my background, Lauren?"

She didn't understand where this was leading, but she answered, anyway. "I know that you're a self-made man. I know you received a scholarship for your education and that you were considered something of a child prodigy in mathematics."

"I come from the shoddiest slums of Philadelphia," he said bluntly. "I was, still am and probably always will be a product of the street. I was in trouble with the police before I was ten years old. If it hadn't been for someone I met...someone who saw potential there and helped, I'd still be on the streets, scrabbling for enough money to buy food, or worse...."

His voice trailed off, leaving him staring off into the middle distance, oblivious to her presence. He was dealing with a painful memory. She could only wait.

This time it was she who reached across the table to cover his fingers with hers. "Is there something else?" she asked gently.

Richard shook his head to clear it, to free his mind of the ugly memories. He started to tell her the rest, but changed his mind. He couldn't deal with any more right now. "Isn't that enough?" he grated.

Lauren gave him a weak smile. There was more; she knew that instinctively.

He misinterpreted the smile. Resolution firmed his jaw, and he shook her hand off with an impatient movement. "I didn't tell you this to get your sympathy. I just wanted you to understand why I might be afraid to entrust my feelings to someone."

Suddenly Lauren understood completely. He had trusted her with his feelings, and she had disappointed him in the worst way possible. She had betrayed that trust by valuing his worth as a person less than his qualifications to be the father of her children.

"Richard, I'm sorry," she said, her voice hardly a whisper. "I'm so sorry. You must hate me." She stumbled, getting to her feet. She had no idea where she was going, but the urge to move, to escape those accusing silver eyes, was overwhelming.

His hand came out to grip her forearm. "Sit down," he said quietly. "I don't hate you, Lauren. Heaven help me, I wish I could."

When she was seated again, he went on. "I don't know if anything can be salvaged from this fiasco or not, but we're going to see." His tone of voice was grim.

Lauren didn't hold out much hope.

THE REST OF THE MORNING passed on turtle's feet. Lauren was subdued, mulling over all he'd said, trying to reconcile the street kid with the suave, self-assured man she knew. She had been content to let Richard set the pace after they left the restaurant and ambled toward the main street that bisected the town of Saratoga Springs.

They strolled up one side of the wide boulevard, aptly named Broadway, and down the other. They browsed in the small boutiques and art galleries, and gradually their conversation became easier, more relaxed. When he laughed at something she said, she breathed a sigh of relief.

At one point, they discovered they shared a passion for skiing. "Lake Placid is less than an hour away," she told him enthusiastically.

"Now if it were only winter instead of summer, we'd be set," he said dryly.

Lauren just stopped herself from saying they could ski next January. Who knew where they would be next January? She slid her hand into Richard's, anyway.

He gave her a flickering glance, but kept her hand firmly in his. Soon the warmth began to build between them again. The linked fingers became arms entwined. The conversation became soft husky laughter as one of them pointed out a particularly gaudy example of a racing season souvenir.

They returned to the race course at one-thirty to join her parents in their clubhouse box.

In the third race Last Bid lived up to all of Slade's claims for him, but only paid even money. Shortly thereafter Red and Sarah left the track to dress for yet another party. "Aren't you going with us this time?" Sarah asked her daughter.

Richard nudged Lauren and she replied, "We're going to stay in town for the harness races, Mother."

"Smart man," said Red. "I told you not to let yourself get caught up in all this partying. You'll be better off sticking with the horses."

When they were gone Richard sat back in his chair and grinned. He looked very much like a fox. "Who do you like in the next race, Wilding?"

Lauren eyed him with mock exasperation and then laughed. He was much too sexy when he was relaxed, much too sexy. "I haven't the slightest idea, Gannon. Who do you like?"

He pretended to muse over the racing form in his hand. "Mmm. Skinny Dip looks good to me," he said. "At least she was good last night."

Lauren laughed and grabbed the paper from his hand. "You fraud! No one would name a horse Skinny Dip."

But someone had. They both bet on the filly and she paid eight to one.

7

"DEE?" Lauren circled the Queen Anne desk, searching for the notes she'd made for her secretary. The telephone cord caught on the corner of the desk, barely missing the ceramic giraffe and a dozen other things Sarah treasured.

She freed the coil, only to have it immediately entangle itself with her mother's inkwell. She caught the silver and crystal antique just before it hit the floor. Thank heavens it was dry.

"Lauren? Is that you?"

She finally found the notes. "It's me. I'm having a battle with mother's inkwell." The cord curled lovingly around the quill. "Hold the phone." Longing for the uncluttered expanse of her office desk, she plucked the feather from the spiral before it could be demolished and set the inkwell on the floor. "Now." She settled back in the chair. "What's going on?"

"Business as usual," answered her secretary lightly. "Did you get the package I sent you?"

The large box was open on the desk before her, spilling its contents and adding to the clutter. Lauren picked up one offending item. "That's why I'm calling. Tell Alexander, absolutely no mink-lined booties."

Dee chuckled. "He was afraid you might feel that way. That's why he told me to check. But he also made me promise to beg."

"Begging won't do a bit of good in this case. Good Lord, how would you wash them?"

"I asked. He informed me that you'd have them cleaned. Any good furrier could do the job." Dee mocked the British accent of Lauren's head buyer.

Lauren smiled into the phone. She could always depend on her secretary, who had two children of her own, to ask the practical questions for her. "A definite no on the mink-lined booties, but you can soothe his feelings by telling him I love the christening dress."

Dee's voice softened. "Isn't it exquisite? I'd almost have another baby to see it christened in that dress."

Lauren fingered the delicate lace and hand embroidery. "The price is outrageous, but I think it will sell. Tell Alexander I'm keeping the sample," she added offhandedly.

There was silence on the line for a minute. "Okay," said Dee finally. "Your sister's pregnant, isn't she?"

"Yes."

"Since you brought it up, there's a rumor going around down here."

Lauren sat bolt upright. "Since I brought what up? Pregnancy? I can assure you I'm not pregnant."

"No. The rumor is about you and Philadelphia's most eligible bachelor being engaged."

Lauren laughed. If there was a hint of distress in the sound, Dee didn't notice. "How did we get from a christening dress to an engagement?" But Dee knew very well that she'd been seeing Richard; there was no point in denying it. "If you want anything for National Secretarys' Week, you'd better not confirm any rumors." Her voice dropped a level. "We're at the negotiating stage, that's all."

She could almost see Dee clapping her hands with glee. Her secretary had been telling her for years she should find a nice man and settle down. "Delores..." Her voice now held a warning.

"I won't say a word. I promise."

Lauren relaxed. "Okay, enough of that. Now about the dress. First, I want you to get in touch with the advertising staff. I'd like to do something along the lines of... 'Begin your own family tradition. This exquisite dress will still be lovely for your great-grandchildren.' We'll have to approach the customer with the idea of generational continuity if we want them to pay that kind of price. Another thing, I'm sure Alexander arranged exclusivity, but it won't hurt to double-check. I would hate to see the dress turn up on sale at Bonwit's. If Alexander can arrange delivery, let's plan to start the ad campaign after Christmas. Say mid-January." She smiled to herself. Spring was the busiest time of the year in her business. "We can try to interest the June brides who've become mothers-to-be."

"Will do. Anything else?"

Lauren hesitated. "You're sure everything's going okay?"

"Relax, boss. Enjoy your vacation. You haven't taken one in years."

"Maybe that's why I'm feeling so cut off. Can't you find even one little crisis that needs my attention?"

"Nope," answered Dee. "Just continue with your negotiations. And call me if a treaty is signed."

Lauren hung up the phone and slid down in the chair, which wasn't designed for that kind of semireclining posture. She thought about her secretary's comment. An agreement had certainly not been reached, but the negotiations had gone well this weekend. But a treaty? A treaty indicated a cessation of hostilities. Richard had been a wonderful lover and an entertaining companion, but he definitely was holding himself back, waiting for something. Occasionally she would glimpse an expression that made her feel as though she were under inspection.

The telephone rang, jogging her out of her reverie. "Hello."

"Good morning."

The mere sound of his deep baritone roused her. "Good morning, Gannon," she answered somewhat breathlessly.

"Busy?"

She looked at the littered desk before her. "Not really. I just got off the phone with my secretary. Seems they don't need me down there, after all." She chuckled. "Except to veto the purchase of mink-lined booties."

She could almost see his blank look when he said, "Run that by me again."

"My buyer tends to get carried away occasionally. How about you? Is Gannon Consultants on the verge of bankruptcy because of your neglect?"

On the other end of the long distance line Richard hesitated for a moment. He almost wished it were. Then he'd know how she really felt about him. "They're limping along. In fact, I thought I'd come up tomorrow, instead of waiting for the weekend."

"Richard! That would be wonderful. Can you really get away for that long?"

"Your enthusiasm is reassuring," he said dryly.

Lauren squeezed her eyes tightly shut. She opened her mouth to speak, not sure what was going to come out, but he interrupted, anyway.

"Doesn't the yearling sale start tomorrow?"

So he wasn't coming up because he couldn't wait to see her. Well, at least he was coming. "Yes. Slade said to tell you he'd made arrangements for you to attend."

"And you," he said firmly. "I want you with me."

"Me? Why?"

"Correct me if I'm wrong. Weren't we going to spend time together? Outside the bedroom?"

"Well, yes, but . . . the tickets are very hard to come by."

"I'm sure Slade can manage to find one more. That is, if you really want to go."

"I'll ask him to try."

"Okay. I'll be in around six. Will you meet me?"

The last question was delivered in a lower voice; it definitely held a sensual suggestion. A shiver ran down her spine and she decided to give him a dose of his own medicine. "Oh, yes," she said, making her voice deliberately husky. "I'll be there."

His hesitation was infinitesimal. "Good. I'll see you tomorrow."

"Tomorrow, Gannon."

Lauren replaced the receiver. For a long time she sat staring out the window, thinking. She toyed with a pencil, turning it end over end until the paper before her was covered with hundreds of tiny little dots. Mr. Gannon, she decided, was in for a few surprises this weekend.

RICHARD'S GREETING when he emerged from the gleaming jet was sufficiently warm and hungry to reassure Lauren, but he was also obviously distracted as he loaded his suitcase in the Jeep.

"Is something wrong?" she finally asked when they were halfway home.

"Mmm? No, nothing that concerns you," he said too abruptly.

Lauren winced.

"I'm sorry. I didn't mean that the way it sounded." He sighed and rubbed a hand over his jaw. "You remember my telling you about the youngster I was involved with through the Big Brother program?"

"Of course I remember. Jay—wasn't that his name? Do you mean you haven't found him yet?"

He shook his head. "No, damn it. I'm really beginning to become alarmed. Staying a few days, even a week or two, with one of his buddies is one thing but . . ." He raked a distracted hand through his hair.

"How long has he been gone?"

"Almost three weeks. I've been searching for him since the end of July. My contacts have come up with nothing." He paused. "Finally I had to bring the police into it. I didn't like to do that."

"Surely they have the best resources."

"Right. But kids like Jay have an inbred resistance to authority. It may do more harm than good. And I may lose credibility with him."

"He means a lot to you, doesn't he?" she asked softly.

"I've been working with him for two years."

"He's lucky to have you to care."

"Lucky?" The word came out on a disbelieving laugh. "Yes, I guess you could say that—just as I was lucky. I see so much of myself in him."

Richard's interest and his dedication to working with deprived youngsters was understandable in light of his own background. Such selflessness enhanced his appeal tremendously as far as Lauren was concerned. He, who had been given a chance, wanted to give something back. Her respect for him and for his accomplishments soared.

He was watching her closely. "I didn't tell you all about myself last weekend. I lived about three blocks from where Jay's mother lives," he added, his voice cold and unfeeling. "His mother has a lot in common with mine, too. She's a prostitute. I was luckier than Jay, though. My mother didn't stick around—I was twelve when she left. I later found out she had died."

The callous way he'd admitted the facts told Lauren more than the words how deeply he had suffered, was still suffering. She felt stunned and paralyzed for a moment. She glanced over at him.

"Watch the road."

Feeling a sudden urge to cry, she bit her lips to stop them trembling. This strong man would be furious at any sign of pity. But to grow up carrying such burdens—it was inconceivable to her. When she thought of the contrast between them she had to blink furiously against the tears. She'd had a family generous with love; she'd had every opportunity to succeed. And he'd had to claw his way to the top.

Richard watched with a sad kind of resignation as the expressions—shock, questioning, then misgiving—chased across her face. He shouldn't have hit her with it like that, he chastized himself. He should have prepared her for it somehow, knowing that to a woman like Lauren the sordid details of his background would naturally be horrifying.

Staring straight ahead through the mud-spattered windshield, Lauren steered the Jeep to the side of the highway and stopped with a jolt. Her hands were clenched on the wheel in a white-knuckled death grip. She let out her breath in an audible sigh and lowered her forehead to her hands.

"The truth is I was arrested fourteen times before I was ten," he added almost apologetically. "For everything from theft to assault with a deadly weapon."

Lauren wondered why there should there be the slightest hint of apology in his voice. It almost made her angry; he deserved nothing but credit. When she turned to meet his dispassionate gaze her eyes were bright with unshed tears. She said nothing, fearing the dam would burst; besides, she didn't know how to put what she was feeling into words. All she knew was that she was wildly, passionately in love with Richard Gannon!

She had misread herself and her feelings so completely and for so long that she could hardly believe it. Her eyes roamed his face hungrily, lovingly—every line, every crevice. How important that face was to her!

Richard didn't believe what he thought he saw in her eyes. "Not a pretty background to hand down to the crown prince is it?"

"Crown . . . I don't understand."

"This child you're so anxious for, that you've gone to such trouble to produce."

At the mention of her original intention and the bitterness that still tinged his words, a tear escaped. All she wanted to do was throw herself in his arms and sob out her pain for the little boy who'd been born angry. She realized even more vividly the extent of the hurt she'd inflicted on him with her damnable manipulation. A man with that background would naturally be cautious and wary. She managed to catch back the sob that followed the tear.

The single drop that trailed down her cheek, sparkling in the late afternoon sunlight, was Richard's undoing. "Ah, hell, Lauren. Turn this thing around and take me back to the airport. If you hurry we can catch the plane before they finish refueling."

"I don't want you to go," she said immediately.

"I didn't tell you the story to get your pity. Damn it, I won't accept it!"

"It isn't offered!" she shouted back. "You still don't know me do you? Look at me, Gannon. Do you see pity in my face?"

He stared, desperately trying to read her emotions. "I don't know what I see," he admitted hoarsely, helplessly.

She felt the rest of the tears fall, making way for a growing anger. "Well, I can guarantee you that it isn't pity."

"Why are you crying, then?"

"I'm not crying anymore! Those are old tears. What you see in my face might be sorrow, or grief for the anguish a little boy must have suffered, but that child isn't you. How could I feel anything but admiration and respect . . . anyway it would be awfully difficult to pity . . ."

"No," he groaned, suddenly understanding his mistake. He clamped a hand at the back of her neck to draw her across the seat.

"Such a pigheaded, stubborn—"

The rest of her words were muffled against his broad chest. His arms were tight and strong. If he trembled it was with the emotional strain of the moment. "Lauren, honey . . ." He sought her mouth, and she lifted her face toward him willingly.

The kiss was different from any they had shared, as though the relationship itself had changed. They had reached a new level of understanding and emotional closeness, and they both sensed it. The kiss was wonderful, thought Lauren hazily. She wanted to know everything there was to know about this man who had taught her what love could be.

When Richard raised his head, a smile was spreading across Lauren's face. "Thank you for telling me everything, Richard."

He frowned. "It isn't a nice story," he stated.

Lauren had anticipated that frown, but it didn't bother her. "No, it isn't a nice story. But I don't think you would have told me if you weren't beginning to trust me."

The wariness was back in his eyes in an instant. Lauren could have kicked herself—and him. Herself for assuming too much; him for being so blind. He ought to know, she thought irrationally; he ought to be able to see that she loved him. Still she held her tongue. When she told him she loved him she didn't want to be faced with a circumspect response. She wanted a genuine reaction that would give her answers. If he reacted as she hoped he would, the shadows between them would be banished forever, leaving nothing but honesty in their place.

For once everyone was at home for dinner, and for once Lauren was impatient with all of them. What happened to the parties? Tonight she would have liked to be alone with Richard.

His eyes made promises, however, which calmed her restless impatience. Later, they said.

She was electrified by the message in those eyes.

RICHARD'S ARM RESTED along the back of Lauren's seat. He appeared casual, but she could see the gleam of anticipation in his eyes as the auctioneer read off the hip number of the next horse offered for sale.

Last night at dinner Slade had described this horse enthusiastically. That was after he and Richard had announced that they'd decided to go into partnership.

Both men had obviously given the matter a great deal of thought. Slade enjoyed a growing reputation among breeders, but there were still those of his peers who considered him a novice in the field. And his playboy image didn't help matters. Even the win by Last Bid, which would boost his stock, wouldn't give him the recognition he was striving to achieve. Slade had been impressed with Richard's knowledge of horses, and his solid reputation in the business world more than made up for the fact that he was a complete greenhorn.

"When did you find time to study horse breeding?" Slade had asked, spooning fresh strawberries from the tray that Shaw passed. A uniformed maid followed with a bowl of thin custard. "Thanks, Maria. I'll pass on the custard."

Richard had shrugged as he, too, helped himself to dessert. "I looked at a couple of books in your father's library last weekend. Most of them had your name in them. They were informative, but I realize there's a lot to learn."

Slade's jaw had gone slack. "You looked at a couple . . ."

"Richard has a photographic memory," Lauren had explained. "Isn't it disgusting?"

Much later, when they lay naked together in the king-size bed, he had brought up the subject of his special ability again. "Aren't you glad I have a photographic memory, love?" he had said. "I can remember that you like this . . ."

"Ah-h-h, yes."

"And you respond when I touch you here . . . and here."

"Richar-d."

"And kiss you . . . here."

NOW LAUREN forced her attention back to the sales pavilion, filled to capacity and humming with tense expectancy. It looked more like a theater than the site for a horse auction. Tiers of red plush seats surrounded the dais on three sides; a green carpeted show stage in the center was surrounded by a white cordon draped between black iron posts. The auctioneer's podium was flanked by two doors—the horses emerged from one and were led away through the other.

The auctioneer, resplendent in a dinner jacket and bow tie, announced the next horse, upon which a groom led in a massive black stallion. Conversation dropped to a whisper as the magnificent animal was presented. Spotlights reflected off his glossy coat, redefining the color with sharp highlights of indigo.

Slade leaned across Lauren to whisper, "You'd better let me do the bidding, Gannon. And whatever you do, Lauren, don't scratch your nose or fan with your catalog or even smooth your lapel."

"I don't have a lapel!" she retorted in a stage whisper, indicating the white sundress she wore. She was as caught up in the excitement as either of them. When the auctioneer began to describe the horse, giving its lineage as well as the stable to which he belonged, Richard reached for her hand.

Slade had cautioned him not to be disappointed if the bidding went too high on this one. There were plenty of other winners in the new crop of yearlings. But she could see, and so could Richard, that this was the one that sparked the excitement in her brother's eyes.

The bidding began low, reinforcing Slade's projection that the horse would go for far less than he felt it was worth. "His sire is underrated," he had told them on the way to the sale. "Underrated, I believe, because of improper handling and training."

Lauren could feel the tension radiating from her brother, but glancing over, she was amazed to see him lift a finger in a casual, unconcerned signal. She intercepted the look Richard gave him, too. His smile was wry as he met her gaze.

A man two rows down lifted his program. She recognized the other bidder with a sinking heart. He was one of the wealthy sheikhs from Maktoum they had discussed. She held her breath. If he really wanted the horse, Richard and Slade wouldn't stand a chance. They were quickly nearing the amount the two men had agreed upon as the limit.

Slade waggled a finger. The man lifted his program and the numbers on the bidding board climbed. Lauren sighed; that was it. Slade wouldn't go any higher. They had lost the horse.

Slade turned to look at Richard. The exchange might have been one made between perfect strangers, but they must have communicated in some way, because Richard calmly signaled the next bid. And the next. She watched, slack jawed, as the bidding progressed. When it was over Lauren was stunned at the amount they had paid.

Amazingly the two men were in high spirits, each taking an arm and lifting her off her feet. Victory was all well and good, she thought in exasperation, but only crazy people would try to compete with oil money! She told them so.

Slade gave her a hug that was meant to be reassuring, but wasn't. "Come on, Sis," he coaxed. "We'll go cool you off with a drink at the Primrose Path. You can start thinking of a name to give our horse."

"Me? I get to name him?" He'd never offered to let her name a horse before.

"Pick something lucky," he advised.

"Slade Wilding, you've lost your mind! That horse would have to win all his races until he was a hundred years old to be worth that much money."

"We'll see," he replied enigmatically.

She looked at Richard in helpless apology and opened her mouth to speak, but before she could get the words out he forestalled her with a squeeze of her arm.

Just then a man approached them, and Richard greeted him in a respectful manner. "How are you, Rashid?"

"I am well, Gannon. And you?"

Richard grinned at the man. "I would have been better had you decided to stop bidding sooner."

"So it was you who was so persistent."

"Me and my partners. May I present Lauren Wilding and her brother Slade."

The sheikh bent low over Lauren's hand. "Such a delightful partner."

Richard slipped his arm around Lauren's waist and pulled her closer possessively. "Slade Wilding is the owner of Wildwood Farms," he told the sheikh.

The man turned to Slade. "Ah, yes. In Kentucky. I have heard of your farm, Mr. Wilding. Perhaps I shall visit with you next year. Maybe you will have something for me, yes?"

"I would be happy to have you," said Slade smoothly, voicing what Lauren decided was the understatement of the year.

"I think I see a table free," said Richard. "If you will excuse us?"

Slade was unaccountably subdued as Richard ordered a bottle of champagne to celebrate. "Something bothering you?" he asked.

"Good Lord, Gannon, I had no idea you traveled in such exalted company. Maybe you should have chosen one of the big boys for a partner on your first venture."

Richard laughed. "I have every confidence in your judgment, Slade. We might have another Man O' War, or even another Secretariat." He shrugged. "But if it doesn't work out, it's still a good tax deduction."

Lauren was appalled that a man who had worked so hard to get where he was could be so cavalier about that much money. Then she realized something about Richard Gannon that she hadn't known before. He was a gambler to the core. He would have enough sense to hedge his bets, but he was definitely a gambler.

Maybe he would take a chance on her. . . .

8

"FEEL LIKE A SWIM?" Lauren asked as the three of them entered the house.

"No, I—" Slade broke off with a chuckle. "You weren't talking to me, were you?"

"I always said you were perceptive—for a brother, that is," Lauren told him sweetly. "Good night, horse trader. Go to bed."

He ruffled her hair. "And just who are you, squirt, to be giving orders to your elders? Maybe I should wake up Mom and Dad to chaperon you."

Lauren shot him a look, and he cowered in mock fear. "I'm going, I'm going." He turned to Gannon and put out his hand. "Good night, partner." He paused, then added, "I hope we're going to be good friends, as well."

Richard shook the proffered hand solemnly. "I think we will. Good night, Slade. Thanks. I've never had so much fun in my life."

"The auction lasts for two more days."

"No, thanks," Richard said with a laugh. "This once was nerve-racking enough. I might forget and scratch my nose or something."

Slade left them. They both watched him go, Lauren with fondness for a much loved elder brother, Gannon with feelings of familial affection he'd never felt for another man. He had friends, but the friendships were usually formed out of a business relationship. For the first time in his life he knew what it would be like if he were really a part of a family. He liked the feeling of belonging.

His gaze met Lauren's. A gentle smile crossed her face, as though she knew what he was thinking. He steeled his heart against letting emotion dictate his actions.

She must have read that thought, as well, because she came to him and wrapped her arms around his waist. "Don't," she murmured. "Don't fortify yourself against me. I'm on your side."

He linked his arms loosely at her waist, studying her features. A smile began and grew, spreading to light his eyes. He dipped his head to taste her lips lightly, then came back for another taste. "Is it too late for that swim?" he asked against her lips.

It may have been late, but Lauren was wide awake and exhilarated. The auction had provided a respite from the tension between them, and she was going to take every opportunity this interval provided. When they were in the pool, relaxed, she was going to tell Richard she loved him. Correction—she was going to convince him of it. "It's never too late," she said with an urgent sincerity.

"Is something wrong?" he asked quietly.

"No, nothing." She shook her head, one brief sharp shake to reinforce her words. But she was afraid. Maybe he wouldn't believe her. The thought was devastating.

"Sure?"

She smiled. "I'm sure." They turned as one and walked down the long hall to the doors leading to the pool. "You really enjoyed the auction, didn't you?" Lauren took refuge in small talk to gain some time; she needed to get her jumbled thoughts in order.

"I really did," he answered, dipping his head to nuzzle a spot just below her ear. His hand slid from her waist to the outer curve of her breast. "I haven't had a lot of time in my life for hobbies, but since getting to know the Wildings I've discovered a couple that could become habit-forming."

His fingers were plucking at her tie belt, and she felt the familiar weakness in her knees. "I suppose we ought to wear bathing suits this time."

The expression on Richard's face made her laugh. "There are other people in the house tonight," she reminded him.

They stepped through the double doors into the shadows beyond. The smell of chlorine assailed her nose at the same time she heard the gentle slap of water against tile.

"Forget the swim. Let's go to bed." Richard's words echoed hollowly in the dark chamber.

Lauren felt for the light switch. Suddenly everything was bathed in subdued light. She reached down to slip her high-heeled sandals from her feet. "Let's swim for just a few minutes. I'm stiff from sitting so long."

"Need a little exercise, do you?" he teased. His hands massaged her neck and shoulders even as he nudged her along toward the pool.

Lauren stretched her neck sensually. "Umm, that feels good. I was afraid to move at the auction for fear I'd buy a horse."

Richard stopped her forward motion, his hands on her upper arms. He kissed the pulse point just under her jaw. She felt him smile against her skin. "I thought you hated exercise."

"Oh, I do," she said, letting her head fall back to rest on his chest. Grinning over her shoulder, she met his eyes. Their smoky depths glowed with tenderness, sending her heart up to her throat. "I'll just swim widths," she added.

Five minutes later Richard emerged from the men's dressing room to find Lauren already in the pool. Sure enough, she was swimming the width rather than the length, covering the distance in five strokes, then turning to swim another five. He couldn't keep from smiling.

When Lauren felt the water surge around Richard's dive, she stopped at the edge of the pool. Treading water, she watched the powerful arms slice a path toward the far end, then back. He swam several fast laps before detouring toward her.

"Very good," she praised laughingly when he reached her side. "Did you ever think about trying out for the Olympics?"

The water was too deep for her to stand, but not for Richard. He put his hands on the coping, one on either side of her head, effectively fencing her in. One of her legs brushed against his, sending a shaft of desire through him. He pushed a wet strand of hair behind her ear; his fingers lingered to cradle her cheek. "You're so beautiful," he said in a low voice. He caught his breath at the shine that suddenly lit her eyes. At this moment she looked very much like a woman in love. His heart began to pound in his chest at the thought.

"I'm glad you think so," she murmured, grasping his shoulders for support and tilting her head into his palm. "Come here and let me kiss you," she directed.

A brow arched amusedly. "Are you going to be aggressive?"

Her blueberry eyes sparkled. Mouth spread into a close-lipped smile, she pretended to weigh the idea. "I'm considering it. What do you think? Shall I?"

The blood in Richard's veins picked up speed and heat as it rushed through to his heart. "I think . . . please," he rasped. One of his hands went to her hip to lift her slightly, molding her against his arousal.

She made a small satisfied sound deep in her throat and wound her legs around him. Her arms circled his neck. She kissed his eyes very softly, her lips like butterfly wings. Slowly she moved to his cheek, across his nose, down to his jaw and finally over the sensual curve of his mouth, her tongue lightly darting in and out between his parted teeth.

Suddenly Richard groaned and pulled her closer, his mouth meeting hers to issue his own challenge. Passion flared, instant and full grown in them both, demanding fulfillment.

Lauren forgot where they were, forgot everything in the throbbing heat of his body surrounding her, stimulating and soothing at once.

Richard's hand at her back sought the tie to her bikini top, but he encountered no knot. He wrenched his mouth away. "How do I get this blasted thing off?" he growled.

Before she could answer, he found the ribbon between her breasts and was working the knot loose. He held her away, his eyes feasting greedily on her full breasts, buoyed by the water. "Oh, love," he breathed, then lifted her slightly to take one of the hard, pink nipples into his mouth.

Lauren plunged her hands into his thick hair, holding him fiercely against her. With a shuddering sigh, she let her head fall back.

A knock on the door provoked a vicious curse from Richard, a weak denial from Lauren.

Richard eased her down until her breasts were below the water line and wrapped his arms protectively around her. She was trembling like an aspen in the wind. "Shhh, " he soothed in a whisper. "Yes?" he said in a louder voice.

Slade's rueful features were suffused with rosy color. "I'm sorry to, uh, intrude. But there's a phone call for you, Gannon. Your secretary. Says it's important."

"Thanks, Slade. I'll be right out."

Her brother nodded, and the door slid shut behind him.

Richard placed a tender kiss on Lauren's brow and released her.

"What atrocious timing!" She dropped her forehead to her hands where they gripped the edge of the pool and started to giggle. When she heard the hysteria in her laugh, she forced down the remaining traces of desire. "Did you get the impression poor Slade was relieved to get out of here?" She turned to face him, and her smile faded. "Richard, what's the matter?"

"Lauren, I'm going to have to leave."

"Well, of course. Go make your phone call. I'll be right here when you get back." She slid her hand to his nape and pulled his head down for a kiss.

He squeezed her shoulder in comforting way, but his kiss was too controlled. She drew back, not understanding. In his eyes she saw contrition, which confused her even further. She fumbled with the ribbon ties at the front of the bikini, but her fingers refused to function. Tenderly Richard took over the task.

When she was covered he explained. "Honey, Roxy wouldn't call, especially at this time of night, if it weren't an emergency. And I'm very much afraid it concerns Jay."

Lauren swallowed her disappointment. "Hadn't you better go see?" she suggested in the same gentle tone he had used. "I'll get us some robes."

Suddenly she was pulled against him. His mouth came down in a hard kiss of hunger and frustration. He lifted her to the side of the pool and hoisted himself up beside her, cursing in colorful and imaginative language.

She stood beside him in her father's study. They were both wrapped in long white terry robes. Richard was gripping one end of the towel he had draped around his neck. The conversation was brief, but Lauren had only to listen to Richard's side to know that the emergency was going to require his presence in Philadelphia.

He replaced the receiver and turned to look at her. "I'm sorry, honey. Really sorry."

"You have to go right now?"

"As soon as I dress and pack. Roxy sent the plane before she called me." He dragged a hand through his wet hair. "Jay's in some kind of trouble. She didn't know what it was, but the police are involved."

"At least they found him," Lauren offered encouragingly.

He wrapped his arms around her, burying his face in her wet tangled hair. "Thank you for being so understanding, sweetheart."

"Richard, I have an idea. Why don't you bring the boy back here?"

He began to shake his head before she'd finished the sentence. "No, no and no," he said firmly.

"Why not? It would do him good to get out of the city. There's certainly enough to do here to keep him entertained. He can ride and swim." Her eagerness grew as she elaborated. "We can take him to the races. And there's a concert—Bruce Springsteen, I think— at the Performing Arts Center. The tickets are as scarce as hen's teeth, but surely mother could get some—"

He continued to shake his head, but his smile grew wider. "Lauren, Lauren. You're very sweet, do you know that?" he interrupted.

She wrinkled her nose. "I'm not sweet at all."

"Okay, you're not sweet. But you're sexy as hell. And back to the original subject—it wouldn't work."

Lauren was still trying to convince him when he snapped his suitcase shut and lifted it off the guest room bed. He had dressed in khaki pants and a white shirt, sleeves turned back to the elbows. He picked up a navy blazer. "Darling, you just don't understand what kind of kid we're talking about here.

Lauren folded her arms across her breasts. "Richard, I do have nephews. I know how boys are."

"Honey, compared to Jay your nephews are angels."

"Maybe on the streets of Philadelphia, but here—" she encompassed the whole of the place with a sweep of her arm "—maybe he would be different. This might be a wholesome change for him." When he still looked as though he would argue, she went on, "Richard, please, at least think about it."

"You always seem to be ordering me to think about something." He pushed back a damp strand of hair from her cheek, tucked it under the towel she had wrapped turban style around her head. "The last time it was marriage." His hand slid to her neck, imprinting her with a warm palm. "About that—"

She silenced him placing two finger across his lips. "That can wait," she said quietly. "We have lots of time to straighten ourselves out. But Jay may not have that much time."

Slade knocked on the open door of the guest room. He was dressed in jeans and a knit shirt. "I'll take you to the airport when you're ready, Gannon."

"I'm dressed." Lauren indicated her own hastily donned jeans. "I'll take him."

"Stay here, sweetheart. I'll go with Slade."

She frowned. "You're just afraid I'll wear you down."

"I agree with Lauren, Gannon. It probably would be a good idea to bring the boy here."

When both Lauren and Richard turned to him in surprise he grinned. "It was difficult not to overhear your discussion. I'll bring the Jeep around front."

Grateful for the unexpected ally, Lauren turned back to Richard. "See. Even Slade agrees. Jay is a part of your life, Richard. I want to know him. Please bring him here."

"You have a generous, loving heart," Richard murmured almost to himself. He thought he'd been in love with this woman before, but the feelings he'd had then seemed trivial compared to the overwhelming emotion that encompassed him now.

His eyes must have reflected that emotion, because Lauren suddenly warned very softly, "Richard, don't put me on a pedestal again. I'll only fall off."

Arms around her, he brought her close, but not too close. If he began to make love to her again he'd never get out of here. He kissed her lightly. "Tell you what. Talk to your mother and father about Jay. I'll think about it and call you tomorrow."

9

IT WAS A SHAME Marsh and Regina weren't as nice as their children, thought Lauren as she pulled up the emergency brake and grinned at her nephews. "Yes, he'll be here through the weekend. No, we can't eat at McDonald's—Grandmother has a lovely dinner planned. And yes, you can be the first to show him the pool and the stables and the tennis courts."

The boys answered with groans that told her quickly which of the suggestions had been the most important.

"Well, at least we get to see the planes," said Wally, ever the optimist. "When I grow up I'm gonna be a pilot."

"Last week you were going to be a treasure hunter," observed Chip.

Wally ignored him. "Boy! Look at that blue one over there."

They piled out of the Jeep, and the heat wrapped around them like a wool blanket. Lauren dug into her shoulder bag to take some coins from her wallet. "Here, have a soda on me. It's hot today."

"Great!" said Wally.

"Thanks, Aunt Lauren," answered Chip with the dignity befitting a twelve-year-old. He was too serious, thought Lauren. She was relieved when he seemed to drop some of the stiltedness and went racing after his younger brother.

Fifteen minutes later she watched intently as another young boy descended from the Lear jet, ahead of Richard. This one was small for his age—not much larger than Chip, though he was four years older. There the resemblance ended. There was not one sign of childhood on his sullen face. Eyes as dark as his black hair were moody and dangerous. His hands were jammed into the pockets of noticeably new jeans; his well-developed shoulders under a gaudy T-shirt were sloped at a deceptively harmless angle. Though she outweighed him by at least twenty pounds, Lauren decided she would hate to meet him in a dark alley.

Richard had stuck to his guns at first. He'd called early that morning to say that Jay was being held in a juvenile detention hall. As soon as he could arrange for the boy's release and get him settled he would return to Saratoga Springs, but it might take a few days. He'd called back just before noon to tell her all hell had broken loose. The police wanted the boy off the streets. The judge had removed him from his mother's custody and was threatening to sentence him. "Lauren, I've asked for temporary guardianship. It was the only thing I could do under the circumstances."

He had sounded harassed and exhausted. "Of course it was, Richard. Do you think you'll be successful?"

"The judge has the idea under advisement right now. After lunch he'll announce his decision."

"Have you eaten or slept at all?"

His answer had been a tired sigh. "I'm going home now to grab a shower and change clothes before court reconvenes."

"Try to eat something, too."

He had chuckled at that. "Yes, ma'am."

"If the judge grants your guardianship you must bring Jay here.... Today," she had added firmly.

Still he'd hesitated.

"I want to see you."

He had inhaled sharply. "And I want to see you. Last night left me with an ache." His deep voice had rolled over her like a morning mist off the mountains.

"Me, too," she had whispered.

Now Lauren walked out onto the tarmac to meet them. She looked first to Richard, lifting her face for his kiss, touching his cheek. She could see what kind of night and day he'd had. A variety of emotions swelled in her breast—tenderness, admiration, concern—but the yearning flame of passion had been relegated to a back burner for now. Her greatest desire was to relieve the tension in his bearing, to nurture and support him. Now she knew that this was the kind of love Richard had felt for her when he'd asked her to marry him. It was the kind of love he'd taught her to feel. "You look tired," she murmured.

"You look gorgeous," he responded, moving his hand restlessly over her back.

She turned to the boy. His stance, his demeanor, his expression—everything about him—was so aggressive that she flinched inwardly at the sight. She wondered if this boy, with enough caring, could overcome a lifetime of deprivation and become as fine a man as Richard. Or perhaps Richard was an extraordinary exception. "Hello, Jay. We're happy to have you here."

He gave a dry, unbelieving laugh—far too worldly a sound for a boy—and muttered, "Thanks." Insolently his dark gaze swept over Lauren, lingering longest at her breasts, which were outlined clearly under the casual white knit shirt. "Hey, Gannon. You've done all right for yourself. She's not a bad broad."

The muscle in Richard's jaw gave a jump. Before he could speak, Lauren linked her fingers in his and squeezed. She put on a warm smile and used all the sincerity she could muster to answer the obnoxious comment. "Thank you, Jay. To an old woman of thirty-one, that's quite a compliment. Shall we go?"

Richard stopped for a word with the pilot, who had already unloaded their bags, just as Wally came running up, followed at a slower pace by his brother. "Hi. You must be Jay. I'm Wally and this is my brother,

Chip. His real name's Marshall, for our Dad, but we call him 'Chip,' for chip off the old block.''

Richard rejoined the small group. He and Lauren exchanged smiles, but neither of them attempted to interrupt. If anyone could ease the tense, forbidding atmosphere, it would be the ebullient Wally.

"Richard, may we see the inside of your plane?" he asked. "Please?"

"Of course you may." He scanned the area, but the pilot had disappeared. "Jay, why don't you show the boys around inside the plane?"

Jay responded to the request by staring at the smaller boy as if he'd come out from under a rock. For Chip he didn't even spare a glance. The silence was heavy, but finally he shrugged carelessly, turned and climbed back into the plane, leaving them to follow or not as they pleased.

They looked to Lauren, who nodded, and they both scampered after the older boy.

Richard dropped his arm across her shoulders, pulling her near. "What a night!" he muttered under his breath. He put his lips to her temple and inhaled deeply. "You smell so good."

"You're exhausted," she observed again, concerned. "Did you get any sleep at all?"

"Not a wink," Richard said. He crooked his arm and lifted her face with a fist under her chin. He studied her features greedily before dipping his head. "And I don't plan to get any tonight, either," he said against her mouth. Her breath was warm and fresh. His tongue slid inside her parted lips with a sigh of home-coming, renewing the taste of her.

Wally's voice brought them back to the present. "We asked Aunt Lauren to take us to McDonald's, but she wouldn't. Hey, Richard, I really like your plane."

Reluctantly Richard lifted his head, giving her a rueful smile. "I'm glad you do," he told Wally. "I'll take you up sometime."

Wally hooted in delight.

Lauren's own smile died under the malevolent gaze she received from Jay. He didn't like her, not one bit. She took a long breath. "Are we ready to go now?" she said brightly.

Jay sauntered off while Richard picked up his suit-case. "Jay."

The boy looked back over his shoulder, but didn't turn. "Yeah?"

"Your bag, Jay," Richard said firmly.

"I'll get it for you, Jay." The words were the first spoken by Chip.

"I'll help," Wally added..

Jay seemed to like their deference. The indolent grin was his first sign of approval since he'd stepped off the plane, thought Lauren sourly, unless you counted his approval of her figure.

Richard's jaw was clenched, but he must have de-cided that at that point a reprimand would have been unproductive.

Lauren admired his control. She would have made the boy get his own bag.

Then she scolded herself for her judgmental attitude. Richard knew him better than she did. This young man had had sixteen years of a savage upbringing. Five minutes of kindness wasn't going to undo it. She wondered if five *years* could.

THE WILDING BOYS had been given permission to stay for dinner. Before the meal was over all four adults were grateful for their presence, especially Wally's. Red loved to tease his grandson, saying he could talk the ears off a billy goat. Tonight his verbosity was welcome.

Jay's sullenness threw a pall over the table, and Wally was the only one unaffected. Slade, whose good nature might have helped ease the tension, was out for the evening. If he ran true to form he wouldn't be back until the wee hours.

As soon as the dessert plates were removed Wally bounced up from his chair. "Can we take Jay to see the horses now?"

"Wally?" his grandmother reminded softly.

"Sorry, Gran. May we please be excused? And take Jay to the stables?"

Sarah smiled and looked to Richard.

"Tonight? I don't think so. It's dark outside, and Jay must be as tired as I am," he said pointedly. "Why don't you watch television, instead?"

"Aw, shucks," said Wally. Then he brightened. "What about the pool? Can we go for a swim?"

Red chuckled. "Not right after eating—you know that. Television in the morning room for half an hour. Then you can swim."

"Hey! Aw-ri-ight! Come on Jay, Chip. Let's go."

To Lauren's surprise, Jay went.

Richard closed his eyes for a moment, then rubbed a hand over his face. The tired gesture didn't escape the other three. "Tell us what happened, Richard," urged Red. "How did you find the boy?"

"I didn't find him. The police did. He'd been living in an abandoned warehouse only a few blocks from his mother's apartment. He was caught stealing food at a market."

"Surely the judge wasn't going to send the boy to prison for that!" said Sarah.

Richard smiled a bit sadly. "It wasn't the first time he'd been arrested, Sarah. So far the offences have been fairly minor—vandalism, drug possession, petty theft."

Sarah raised a brow. "Minor?"

Red explained for Richard. "Minor, darling, in comparison to the more violent crimes. Do you think there's a chance for him to straighten out, then, Richard?"

Richard shot him a grateful look and nodded. "I think so. Jay's bright. His grades—when he bothers to go to school—are good, but he's so far behind he needs remedial classes. I'm trying to make arrangements for him to go to a school-clinic in Virginia that has had great success in treating troubled children."

"He'll balk at that," predicted Lauren.

Richard grinned at her. "You read him well. He needs more help than I'm capable of giving him, though. Professional help. I hope I can get him in— they have a waiting list as long as my arm. For the first six months he won't be allowed to leave the clinic. After that he'll be reevaluated." He frowned and toyed idly with his coffee spoon, his eyes uneasy. "His main hang-up is confinement."

The silence that followed his statement was broken finally by Sarah, who glanced at her watch and stood up. "By the time the boys get into their suits, their thirty minutes will be up. I'll go tell them."

"I'll go with you," Lauren offered.

They smelled the smoke before they reached the den. Sarah looked puzzled, while Lauren felt her anger rising. Jay was sprawled on Sarah's favorite chair; the two younger boys sat cross-legged on the floor at his feet. All three of them were puffing away on Red's finest Havana cigars. Jay held his at an arrogant angle between his teeth. Chip was noticeably green, but Wally seemed to be thoroughly enjoying himself.

Lauren restrained her mother with a hand on her arm. "Let me handle this," she said grimly. "Okay, boys, you just forfeited your swim," she told them, marching into the room.

Jay studied her for a minute. "Ah, hell, teach. I wanted to see you in a bikini," he responded very softly, very suggestively. His gaze made the now familiar trip down to her breasts.

Lauren eyed him coolly and squelched the temptation to make a smart remark. She wouldn't offer him a challenge to respond to. Instinctively she knew the best course of action was simply to ignore Jay's attempts to provoke her. Having a verbal battle wouldn't do either of them any good.

She turned to her nephews, who had hastily stubbed out the cigars and scrambled to their feet. "Chip, call your father. Tell him to come get you."

"We can walk," offered Wally.

She glared him down.

"Are you gonna tell him?" asked Chip.

"No, you will do that."

They hung their heads.

Sarah spoke from behind her. "Come along, boys. You can use the phone in the hall."

"Geez! What a cop-out! Why would they rat on themselves?" said Jay sarcastically when they had gone. He took another puff and studied the smoke, which didn't quite make a ring. Then he drank from a glass she hadn't noticed before. The smell was distinctive.

She stood where she was, uncertain how to handle this. The boy had been there only a few hours and already he was smoking her father's cigars and drinking his bourbon. What else would he find to get into before it was over?

Over? It suddenly occurred to her that "it" wasn't going to be over. This boy was important to Richard, a part of his life. If, as she prayed, she became a part, too, she would have to learn to live with Jay. The notion made her pause.

"Because they don't want a lie on their conscience," she finally answered his hypothetical question with a calmness she didn't feel. She reached down to take the cigar and glass from him.

He didn't argue, merely shrugged and stood, meeting her eye to eye, but his glare was definitely hostile. "I'm glad I don't have a conscience." He began to wander the room, picking up a whatnot here and there, examining it and never quite managing to replace the things in their original spots. He picked up the giraffe from her mother's desk.

"I saw one of these in a pawnshop once. It doesn't look like something you'd have with all the other ritzy things around."

Lauren shrugged. "My father won it for my mother at a fair on their first date. It has sentimental value for her. Please put it down."

Jay watched her expression as he tossed the figure in the air and caught it with a casual swipe.

Lauren snatched back a shriek. Every member of the family knew how much her mother loved the little figure. And this smart aleck was treating it like a worn out softball. "I said, put it back," she bit out.

He surprised her by doing just that. He stood there rocking on his heels, his hands jammed into his pockets, that extremely unpleasant smile on his face. "You don't like me worth a damn, do you?" he sneered.

She kept her face expressionless. "I haven't known you long enough to decide whether I like you. Since you've been here you've made a deliberate effort to be obnoxious."

"Wo-o-o!" He shook his fingers in a derisive gesture. "Sixty dollar words! Tell me something, lady. Was it you who got Richard to sic the cops on me?"

She felt Richard's hand on her shoulder. "No," he answered for her. "She had nothing to do with my calling the police. It was my idea. I told you, I've been looking for you for three weeks, Jay. I was worried."

The boy gave a snort of disbelief.

"Jay, I know you must be tired. Why don't you go on up? I'll be along soon." Richard suggested, changing the subject.

The boy surveyed them both with the same insolent stare. "Sure," he said carelessly. He grinned a cocky grin. "Gettin' horny, Richard? I don't blame you. If I had Lauren's hot bod to—"

The unspeakable word was quickly cut off when Richard spun him around by the shoulder. "Apologize. Now!" he commanded.

"Sorry." Jay complied grudgingly.

Richard hesitated briefly, as though he might demand more. Then he marched the boy toward the door. "I'd better show you the way," he said through clenched teeth, "in case you've forgotten."

Lauren took a minute to compose herself before she trailed after them. She was totally confused. On one hand she felt sympathy for the boy and wanted to be of help if possible. On the other she considered him disagreeable and possibly dangerous. She had an awful premonition that someone in this family was going to be hurt, badly hurt, if he stayed here. More than likely that person would be her, but it could be one of her parents or a nephew. She tried to shake off the feeling of dread, but it persisted.

When she entered the front hall, the sight that awaited her caused her to roll her eyes. Her mother and father waited to one side, while Marshall stood toe to toe with Richard. He had a boy by each hand. He was furious.

Evidently her delay had caused her to miss most of the scene, since Marshall seemed to be near the end of his tirade. "Just get him out of this house and back to where he belongs, Gannon, which I would think is jail."

At that moment Red Wilding stepped forward. "Do I have to remind you, Son, that this is my house?" he said to Marshall. "I issue all invitations." He didn't raise his voice; he didn't make any threatening moves. He simply stood casually with his hands thrust into his pockets.

Marshall's face turned even darker red. Without another word he turned and stalked from the house, dragging the boys with him.

"We'll go," said Richard.

"No," countered Red firmly.

Jay's dark eyes darted between Richard and Red as the two men looked at each other. For a fleeting second, so brief as to make Lauren wonder if she'd dreamed it, there was a flash of vulnerability in his expression. Then the sullenness was back. But she'd had that glimpse, and it was enough to affirm that here was a boy who hadn't a notion how to take kindness, he'd had so little in his life. She wondered if he'd ever be able to let anyone beyond the protective wall he had built around himself.

Red crossed to them. He touched Richard's shoulder. "Take him up, son," he said quietly. "You're both exhausted. Things will look different after a good night's sleep." Finally Richard nodded. He and Jay climbed the stairs without another word.

Lauren kissed her mother and father good-night. "I'm going up, too."

Red gave her a tight hug. "That's a fine man. I hope you appreciate him," he said gruffly.

She smiled. "Yes, sir. I do. I'm not so sure about Jay, but I do appreciate Richard." She kissed his cheek again. "You're a fine man, too."

"May I make a suggestion?" put in Sarah.

Red grinned and brought his wife into a three-way embrace. "Of course, my dear. We'd welcome one. You always know what's best for all of us before we know ourselves."

Lauren marveled that the sound of her mother's laughter could be so light after the emotional scene that had just taken place. Sarah kissed her husband's cheek and wiped away the pink lipstick she'd left there. "It's nice to be appreciated. I hope I don't disappoint you. This one is pretty ordinary by my standards. I was just going to suggest to Lauren that she raid your bar and take a medicinal glass of bourbon up to Richard. He looks as though he could use it."

"At the risk of encouraging anyone to make loose with a fine Kentucky sour mash, I have to agree."

Lauren didn't tell him someone else had already made loose with it. When she reached the upper hall, she found Richard sprawled on the sofa, head back, eyes closed. She kept to the carpet runner so as not to disturb him. Quietly she set the glass down and went to stand over him. The lines in his face were pronounced. His hair was rumpled. He had never looked so wonderful to her.

She had to remind herself that things still weren't settled between them. She couldn't make the assumption that he had completely forgiven her just because of the passionate scene in the pool last night. She would never make assumptions about this man again, she vowed. That was how it had all begun—her assuming that Richard Gannon would want to marry her under any conditions, that because he loved her he would be content in the sterile kind of marriage she'd planned. She knew him better now. He had taught her a lot. Sterility was the last thing he would accept in a marriage. It would have to be all or nothing.

With this latest development in the form of Jay, however, she wasn't sure she could live up to his "all," she realized sadly. She had to know what his plans were for Jay, beyond the school in Virginia. Even though she felt sorry for the boy, even though she would take his burden of pain upon herself if it would help, she knew it wouldn't. She was enough of a pragmatist to recognize this was a hurdle to overcome before she and Richard could be married. Jay would need months, years, of constant attention and love. His wall of resentment was built so high and wide only the most patient care could dismantle it. She didn't think she had the ability to do that.

Lauren didn't realize Richard was awake until he reached for her hand and pulled her down on the sofa next to him. His eyes were still closed and his voice when he spoke was full of a weariness that ran bone deep. "I need to explain some things to you."

She smoothed a lock of hair away from his brow. "Not tonight. You're too tired."

Wrapping his arms around her, he buried his face in her hair. "Lord, yes, I'm tired."

"Daddy was right. Things will look different in the morning." She silently prayed that would be so.

He opened his eyes and looked at her. "I won't be here in the morning."

She was surprised by this defeatest attitude, not at all like Richard. It had to be the exhaustion talking. "Gannon, I refuse to listen to a word. Daddy sent you a glass of his best bourbon." She stood up and tugged at his arm to bring him up, too. "You're going to drink it and go to bed. Come on."

He staggered slightly as she took his hand in one of hers and picked up the glass with the other.

"This is important. The situation concerns you, too, Lauren," he said very seriously.

"I know, but I won't listen until tomorrow. Drink this and take your clothes off." Handing him the glass, she left him standing in the middle of the guest bedroom while she went into the bathroom and turned on the taps in the tub.

When she came out she saw that he'd partially obeyed. The level of liquor in the glass was down about halfway and Richard was down to his jockey shorts. She suspected his compliance was purely automatic; he was very definitely out on his feet. Changing her mind suddenly, she crossed to the bed. She lifted the covers, holding them aside. "Forget the bath. You'd probably drown in the tub. Come on, Richard. Get into bed."

He frowned at the pillow in an obvious effort to remember something. His brow cleared. "Aren't you going to sleep with me?"

She laughed softly and shook her head. "Oh, Gannon." He sounded like a little boy himself at the moment. But when he automatically stripped the shorts from his body and fell back on the bed, she was reminded quite vividly that this was no boy.

"Lauren?" His voice was slurred; his eyes were closing slowly.

Tenderly she tucked the covers around him. "I'll be back, Gannon. I'll sleep with you."

He sighed, content.

AFTER A RESTLESS NIGHT next to a man who might as
well have been a bag of cement, Lauren was up early.
After dressing in white cotton pants cropped above
the ankle and a hot pink shirt, she looked in on Richard. He was still sleeping soundly. There was no sound
from Jay's room, or from Slade's.

In the small kitchen at the end of the hall she put on
a pot of coffee. While it perked she went downstairs
to get one of the two papers that were delivered every
morning. One of them was sacrosanct—untouched
by anyone but her father. The other was up for grabs,
and there was usually a wrangle over it.

She brought both papers inside and left one on the
hall table for Shaw to find when he began the prepa-
rations for breakfast. It wasn't until she had reentered
the upstairs hall that she noticed her purse. She always zipped it and she always dropped it on the near-
est horizontal surface. It was hanging by the strap
over the arm of a chair. And it was open.

A cold hand descended to settle on her heart.

LAUREN WAS SIPPING COFFEE and reading the edito-
rials when her brother stuck his head out of the door
to his room. "Aha! I thought I smelled coffee. Would
you bring me a cup, sweet sister?"

"Get it yourself," she said without lifting her eyes
from the page.

"If I do you may be embarrassed," he warned. "I'm not dressed."

Lauren eyed him with suspicion. "Will you promise not to take the paper?"

"Would I do that?" he asked innocently enough for her to believe him. "Richard not up?"

She put the paper aside and rose. "Not yet."

"And the boy? Did he arrive last night, too?" he asked as she passed his door on the way to the kitchen.

She met his sleepy stare. Her steps slowed. Lowering her voice to a whisper, she answered, "Yes, and he's a holy terror, Slade." Her worried eyes betrayed her misgivings. "He's already taught Chip and Wally how to smoke. Daddy's best cigars, no less."

He chuckled. "Did they throw up? That's how I remember my first attempt."

Reluctantly she met his smile. Depend on Slade to put things in perspective. "Chip looked green, but Wally enjoyed himself thoroughly." She frowned again, wondering if she should mention the money that was missing from her purse. "He was drinking, too. We had a real row when Marsh came to pick up the boys."

"I can imagine. Our elder sibling isn't the most tolerant man in town." He waved a bare arm. "Scoot along, sister. I want my coffee."

She was filling a mug, when she heard the telltale squeak of the door. She whirled in time to see her brother, dressed in jeans, dash out to grab the paper off the sofa. "Slade, you rat!"

"You should have taken it with you." He laughed and waved the paper as if it were a victory flag.

They had played at this battle for more years than she could remember. She had her own ammunition. "Coffee," she said in a soft purr as she approached his door. "Rich and strong and hot, just the way you like it." She held the mug toward him, but was careful not to get too close.

He closed his eyes and inhaled the aroma. "Mmm. Does smell good. How about the Life-style section?"

She hesitated. Life-style was a major concession; the crossword puzzle was in there. "Life-style and Editorial," she demanded. "I was in the middle of Buchwald's column."

"Okay. Give me my coffee."

"When I have my Life-style and Editorial."

"We'll exchange at the same time," he decided.

Suddenly a voice intruded on their exchange. "Geez! You sound like a couple of spoiled brats."

Startled, they both turned to see Jay lounging against the wall. Coffee sloshed onto Lauren's wrist. "Ouch. Damn it."

Slade reached for the mug and she put her wrist to her mouth. "You okay?"

She nodded, but tears stung her eyes. The coffee was scalding hot.

Slade turned back to the boy. "You must be Jay. I'm Slade, Lauren's brother." He advanced, holding out his hand.

His offer of a handshake was rudely ignored. "Any more of that?" Jay nodded toward the cup in Slade's hand.

"Wouldn't you rather have milk or juice?" Lauren asked.

He looked at her as if she'd left her brain in Siberia. "No, I don't want milk." He pronounced each word as though she were hard of hearing.

Lauren met his look. "The coffee's on the counter back there. Help yourself," she snapped.

"Be right out," mumbled Slade, and disappeared into his room.

Jay came back and sat down in a chair across from the sofa. He had to move her purse to do so. He juggled it by the strap, watching for a reaction, and stared at her in a deliberate attempt to make her uncomfortable. He slurped his coffee. He belched. Then he set the hot cup down on the walnut table between them, deliberately spilling some and making no move to wipe it up. "Hey," he said.

Lauren held the paper in front of her eyes and ignored him. It was the only thing to do. She wasn't at her best in the morning and she might have slapped the sneer off his face otherwise.

"Hey, you!"

Finally she lowered the paper and looked at him.

"How does it feel to be rich?"

"Feels good," she said. "We don't apologize for what we have, Jay. We've been lucky, but we all work very hard."

His gaze was cold and meant to be intimidating. He repeated the question he'd asked last night. "You don't like me much, do you?"

Jay didn't know that he was talking to a woman who had fought for and gained her place in the business world by refusing to be intimidated by men with chips on their shoulders. "Not one damn bit," she said mildly, and went back to the paper.

In a blaze of fury he jerked the paper from her hands and sent it flying. "I'm talking to you, Miss Rich Bitch!"

"Are you? I thought you were trying to pick a fight."

"You think that just because you've got a lot of money and live in a fancy house you can lord it over us peasants!"

"Is that what you think you are?"

"No, it's what you think I am. You think you're better than me."

Lauren sighed. This had gone far enough. "Maybe I am."

She could tell that her answer shocked him. It rather shocked her, too. "At least I try not to hurt the people who care about me. You don't even try." His furious gaze became a blank stare. She went on. "I told you. I work hard. My father doesn't believe in getting something for nothing."

He snorted. "At least you have a father!"

There it was again—that hint of vulnerability. She hadn't been mistaken the night before.

Her expression softened. "Richard cares about you. Maybe he isn't your father, but he really cares. And you care about him."

"I don't! Not about him or anybody else," he denied bluntly, and the feral smile appeared. "Except for maybe my supplier."

Lauren was perplexed for a minute before she realized what he meant. The realization saddened her more than anything that had gone before. If Jay was heavily into drugs, Richard's ability to get through to him was going to be severely hampered, perhaps made impossible.

"I'll tell you something else, too. I don't like you any more than you like me. Richard says you might get married. I think you'd better decline nicely, Miss Rich Bitch. If you marry him he'll never see me again."

As a threat it was effective. Lauren could hear the death knell of their relationship in his defiant words. "I hope you don't mean that, Jay," she said quietly past the lump forming in her throat. When he didn't answer she asked, "Could you do that to someone who's trying so hard to help you?"

"Oh, Gannon's good for a few bucks every now and then. . . ."

"And me, too?"

His cold eyes pierced her, daring her to mention the money.

"Good morning," said Richard from behind him.

Lauren was relieved to see he was smiling; he obviously hadn't overheard. She wasn't ready for a confrontation—not yet.

"Did you sleep well, Jay?" An additional, wordless communication passed between them, and Jay dropped his head.

"Yeah," he said. "I guess."

Lauren couldn't read their thoughts. She didn't even try. Obviously Richard could handle the boy better than she could. She stood and crossed to him. "Good morning. Do you feel better?"

He hooked an arm around her neck and drew her forward for a lingering kiss. She tried to resist—it wasn't the sort of kiss that was appropriate in front of the boy—but he was intractable. He lifted his head just a fraction. "Now I do," he whispered softly against her lips. "How could you do that to me?"

"Do what?" she whispered back.

"Good morning," Slade said cheerfully, banging the door to his room behind him. He reached down to pick up the sheets of paper Jay had scattered so violently and folded them along with the sections he carried. "I'm starved. Let's go downstairs."

Lauren pulled out of Richard's arms. "I'm hungry, too. How about you, Jay?"

The boy had an odd look on his face, one she couldn't interpret. "Yeah." He appeared strangely subdued.

The three adults looked at him, but none of them commented.

Red and Sarah had just come down for breakfast. At Sarah's request, Shaw had set the table on the terrace. Sunlight sparkled on fine crystal and a light breeze fluttered the tablecloth.

Sarah shook out her napkin. "Don't forget our party tonight. We should all be dressed and down by seven. The guests are invited for seven-thirty, but there are always a few who'll come early."

"Sure, Mom," said Slade cheerfully. "Can I pick up anything for you in town?"

"I'll check my list before you go," said Sarah.

Lauren watched her brother with suspicion. He seldom volunteered for errands and was never this lively in the mornings. Obviously he was planning something.

Sure enough, they had barely finished their melon when, with the voice of authority, he spoke. "I have to go to the track for a short time this morning. I'm going to take Jay with me. We'll have lunch in town."

"I'll go with you," said Red. "The trip will get me out of your mother's way."

Richard met Slade's gaze. "Thanks."

"Hey!" said the boy belligerently. "Don't I have anything to say about this, Gannon?"

He answered Jay calmly and carefully and, Lauren thought, a little sadly. "No, you don't, son, not today. Lauren and I have some things to work out. Some things that can't be postponed any longer. We need to talk . . . alone."

At a loss to explain the sadness in his tone, Lauren was suddenly more apprehensive than ever. She felt Jay's accusing eyes on her. "You remember what I said," he seemed to be telling her. He also seemed perfectly confident that she'd do what he had told her to do earlier that morning.

She met his glare in silence, realizing belatedly that she had been mistaken in not confronting the boy immediately with the theft from her purse. He thought she was caving in to his demands. Possibly she was.

Richard was right. This discussion couldn't be put off any longer. But she dreaded the outcome.

10

RICHARD AND LAUREN drove the Jeep to the spot where the road ended, and then got out to walk. She was taking him to see her parcel of land that overlooked the lake. The path was narrow and overhung with gigantic pines that had laid a carpet of brown needles that muffled their footsteps. Sunlight dappled the way and birds sang an accompaniment. The air smelled fresh and clean, and there was a hint of approaching fall in the breeze that ruffled her hair.

"It isn't much farther," Lauren said over her shoulder. "Just around this next bend."

"I'm enjoying the exercise," Richard said wryly. "Aren't you?"

She turned and, walking backward, made a face.

Just then they emerged into a flat meadow about twenty feet above the lake. Richard set down the picnic basket he'd been carrying and turned slowly, looking out over the vast and dramatic view of the clear blue water, the mountains beyond. "This is fantastic," he said. "Absolutely beautiful. What kind of house do you see here?"

She met his enthusiasm. "Contemporary. Don't you think it calls for a lot of glass to take advantage of the scenery?"

"No question about it. And to watch the seasons change. . . ." He had absently thrown his arm across her shoulders. Now he looked down into her eyes.

"With you," she added tentatively, drawing closer. He looked rested, the lines in his face less pronounced, his eyes clear and brilliant.

He placed his large hand at the back of her head, his gaze roaming over her face. "I had hoped . . . your feelings seem to have changed."

"Oh, yes, my feelings have changed," she said softly.

The flame that suddenly ignited in the gray eyes was hot and hungry. "Will you make love with me? Now?" he questioned, his breath warm and promising at her ear.

She resisted, when all she really wanted to do was melt against him. "We should talk about Jay," she said. "Slade's given us this opportunity. We may not have another."

He ignored her resistance, tightening his arms. "I know. But this is more important right now. I wanted you so badly last night."

"But you were exhausted," she said tenderly.

"I'm not exhausted now. And I want you even more."

She made no further protest when he took the blanket from her. Laughing unsteadily, she pointed to a spot under the branches of a large evergreen. "The best view is from over there."

Richard felt his overwhelming need threaten his sanity. He thought he might die if he didn't have her. He followed and spread the blanket under the tree she indicated. "If you think I'm going to be interested in the view, lady, you're badly mistaken," he said, reaching for her. "Let's not think beyond this minute, love."

As Lauren watched, the sun reached under the branches of the tree to turn his eyes to smoke. "Please, yes. Darling, make love to me." She lay down on the blanket.

Propping himself on an elbow beside her, he smiled slightly and slid his hand beneath her short top to cup her breast. Her nipple responded instantly, growing hard under the satin barrier of her brassiere.

She closed her eyes, the better to relish the compelling sensations that flooded her. Richard's lips came down on hers, warm and soft, cool and firm. The sensation of tongue meeting tongue sent a shimmer of delight through her. As the kiss became more demanding, wave after wave of excitement began to build. Slowly Richard urged her onto her back and rose above her. "I want to undress you, to see your beautiful body bathed in warm sunlight and nothing else."

She made some sound of assent, and he reached for the front snap of her white pants. He lowered the zipper with maddening slowness, spreading open the sides as he went. He dipped his head to leave a tender kiss at her navel, then slid the pants over her hips and down the length of her legs. When he realized her canvas shoes were going to have to come off first, he gave her a rueful grin. "I'm rather clumsy at this."

Her smile warmed. "Good."

The shoes were tossed aside, and the slacks. The scrap of lace that was her panties followed. He took her hand and hoisted her to a sitting position so he could strip the top over her head. The bra came last. By then his hands were trembling noticeably and a fine film of perspiration had formed on his upper lip. Eyes riveted on her breasts, he eased her down on the blanket.

His fingers touched the rosy crests of her nipples as though learning the texture of some fragile exotic flower. "You're such a pretty color. All roses and cream. My skin looks so rough next to yours."

She looked at the contrast of color, his hand and her breast, and thought it was the sexiest thing she'd ever seen. When his hand grasped her, gently squeezing, rotating his palm over her sensitive nipples, she sighed her pleasure and closed her eyes again. He bent to bathe the sweet pink peak with his tongue, to scrape his teeth across her flesh.

Her arms came around his back. "Your turn," she whispered huskily, reaching to pull the tail of his shirt from his jeans.

He got to his feet and began to tear off his clothes. In seconds he was over her again. His lips touched hers, seeking the deepest warmth within. His tongue entered, teased, withdrew, only to enter again.

The warmth of the sun on her face, the scent of grass and pine, the sleepy droning of a bee somewhere nearby, made the whole setting seem like the beautiful world of a sun-blessed fairy tale.

"Look at me," he urged.

She didn't think she could manage the full weight of her heavy lids, but she opened them halfway. Her gaze traveled upward. The sight of his muscular chest and the crisp hair that grew there, the strong chin, the sensual mouth, the eyes that had darkened to the color of iron, all teamed to make her shift restlessly, cry out softly with desire. His hand touched the sensitive flesh of her inner thigh. She arched upward as he entered her in a sure, flowing motion until he filled completely, until he was a part of her body, her soul.

She met his thrusts, her limbs wrapped around him as the pressure built in her.

Suddenly she caught her lip between her teeth. The air was still, still as the blood in her veins, the breath in her lungs. All nature waited, poised on the brink.

Wild sensations ripped through them both simultaneously. He felt her contract around his manhood with a sense of triumphant possession; she felt his life force fill her, and experienced the exultant ecstasy of love.

Richard tenderly stroked the damp hair away from her brow. "I love you, my darling. I love you so," he whispered over and over.

"And I love you," she answered breathlessly, wonderingly. "You've shown me passion I didn't think I was capable of feeling." She spoke the truth. Each time he made love to her it excited, then consumed her. It had never been this way, and would never be with any other man.

They dozed for a few minutes, floating on a dreamlike cloud somewhere in the upper stratosphere. Later they rose and dressed.

Lauren went back for the picnic basket. She sank to her knees on the blanket and took out a thermos of coffee, then set the basket aside. Richard remained standing. "I love this spot," she said, pouring out two cups. "This is where I used to come to write my poetry when I was a romantic teenager."

If there was a trace of the bittersweet in Richard's smile, she knew why, of course. He was thinking about his own teenage years, and Jay's. She plunged right in. "I'm worried, Richard. I'm afraid it won't work."

He didn't hesitate with his response. "I can see it won't. Not like this, but Lauren . . ."

"Come, sit here." She reached for his hand and pulled him down beside her. Leaning against the trunk of the tree, he stretched out his long legs, crossing them at the ankle. He sipped his coffee.

"Richard, I admire what you're trying to do. And I agree that Jay is worth helping. He isn't half as bad as he would like us to believe."

Richard was surprised at her perceptiveness. "You can see that?"

"There've been moments when he couldn't hide his sensitivity. But, Richard, the boy really hates me."

Richard took her hand. Linking their fingers, he studied them for a minute. "I know it appears that way to you, love, but..."

She set aside her cup to grip his hand tightly between both of hers. "He's jealous of our relationship. I can understand that. If I had time—some experience in such things—but I have a business to run and so do you. Who's going to watch him?"

"I didn't say I planned to adopt him."

"That's what it will amount to and you know it. I can't manage a marriage, a career and a rebellious delinquent. One or two, but not all three. It would destroy us, Richard."

"Do you want me to wash my hands of the boy?" he inquired harshly. "Well, I can't. I've got two years invested in believing I can help. I'm committed to him."

Integrity, honesty, moral strength—hard lessons to learn and even harder to live with at times. Richard strongly believed they were the attributes that kept man above the animals. One did what was right, though it might hurt more than the most excruciating physical pain, because not to do the right thing made one a lesser person. His own lessons, learned at a later time in his life than most, were vital to him, because he had lived for so many years without ever having known them. He had been living on a level with the animals.

"No! I wouldn't accept that kind of sacrifice even if you offered it, Richard. Maybe, when he's on his feet...in a couple of years..." She dropped his hand.

"A couple of years?" he exploded. "You expect us to wait a couple of years? What about your plans for a family?"

"I'll just have to settle for nieces and nephews, I guess." She tore off a piece of grass and chewed on it for a minute. "Richard, I hope with all my heart that someday you'll be able to forgive me for what I did." She shook her head impatiently. "I can't believe even now that I could have been such a fool, or planned such a cold-blooded thing."

"Why?"

Her head swung toward him. "Why what?"

"Why can't you believe it?" He wasn't looking at her. His gaze was fixed somewhere out over the lake.

"Well, I...what do you mean?"

He tossed out the contents of the cup. "What has changed that you should be so hard on yourself?" he asked mildly.

She couldn't free her gaze. There was a silent unbreathing moment between them, when words were unnecessary. "You know why," she said softly. "I told you—I love you."

She was pulling him, drawing him closer on invisible strings. He resisted. "You've told me that before.

When we had different definitions of the word. I want to know how you're defining it now."

She reached out to frame his face. Her eyes shone with love and sincerity. "What I feel now is unlike anything I've ever felt before. I was going to tell you last night when we were in the pool."

He smiled tenderly and lifted a handful of her hair. The light shone through as he let the golden silk sift through his fingers, thinking it looked like a section of a delicate, gossamer cobweb. "Was that only last night?"

Two tears rolled gently down her cheeks. She clasped her hands together in her lap. "I love you so much," she whispered, the words echoing on the wind. She shook her head hard. "No, no, that's not enough!" Her voice grew strong. "I adore you. I feel all the desire and passion, the romance and all the tender devotion of a lifetime. I wish I'd known what love was. But it took you to teach me. All those things that I thought were so impractical—I feel all of them."

He reached for her.

"It won't work for us," she protested when his arms came around her, inflexible and unrelenting, to lift her across his lap. She pressed her face against his chest.

He rocked her back and forth in his arms. "It will." The desperation in his voice was to convince himself as well as her. "Don't you know that I would never allow anything to come between us now? I'll make arrangements, he'll have the best care, but I can't let you go."

"You have to. Didn't you see his face? That's what he fears most of all. That I'll take you away from him." Her voice was strangled.

The very qualities that had drawn her to Gannon from the first would be the qualities that called for the end of things—his sense of honor, his duty.

"I'll get him enrolled in that school in Virginia. They have a waiting list, but I'll get him in," he vowed.

She raised her tear-stained face to stare at him. "Oh, Gannon," she breathed sadly. "Do you know how guilty that makes me feel."

"Darling, I didn't tell you to make you feel guilty. I'm not trying to get rid of Jay. Or foist his problems off on somebody else."

"Will he see it that way?" she asked quietly, knowing her words would cause him pain. "When you send him away, will he ever understand, especially if I'm involved? He's very hostile toward me."

"Jay felt strange and uncomfortable in such opulent surroundings." Richard shifted, not quite comfortable with his own explanation.

She sighed. "Richard, I've seen your house in Philadelphia. It isn't exactly a hovel. I presume he's visited you there?"

He nodded.

She considered telling him about the theft now, but decided against it. She would never mention it. The knowledge would make everything harder for Richard, put a further strain on his relationship with the boy. She loved him too much to add to his burden. "Jay hates and resents me," she finally said.

"Damn it, Lauren, I think you're overreacting."

The accusation ignited her anger. "Overreacting? To a teenage brat who looks at me like I'm a side of prime beef?"

"No!" he exclaimed, rejecting her argument.

"Refusing to face the problem isn't going to help, Gannon."

He held her tightly, his mind racing, searching. Something could be worked out. *Something*, he cried out silently, even as he feared the nebulous shape of the future.

But damn it! He deserved happiness, too. He had it right here in his hands. He didn't know if he could bear to let it go, even for a child who deserved his loyalty. A child who desperately needed it. And Jay wasn't really his responsibility; he wasn't the boy's father.

Richard recoiled from his own thoughts, rebuking himself. Just because there was no blood between them didn't lessen the fact that he was responsible. He'd cared about Jay for two years, fought to gain his confidence. If he abandoned him now without having the boy's complete understanding, Jay would never recover. Lauren was wise enough to recognize the fact.

His fingers slid up into her hair. Gripping her head, he forced her eyes to meet his.

Lauren saw the denial there, and the apprehension. She opened her mouth to speak, but he shushed her.

"Let it rest for now. Maybe we'll think of something." Even as he said the words he knew they were a lie.

SOMETHING WAS WRONG. They knew it as soon as they parked in front of the house. The front door was standing wide open. There was shouting from inside, loud angry voices Lauren recognized as her brothers'. She and Richard exchanged glances. He jumped from the Jeep and hit the ground running. She was right behind him.

"What's going on?" Richard demanded of the two angry men facing each other in the entrance hall. Red Wilding stood off to one side. Two strange people— Lauren supposed they were members of the catering staff—were listening avidly from the dining room. There was no sign of her mother, she saw with relief.

Marshall whirled on Richard. "I'll tell you what's going on. My boys have disappeared. That juvenile delinquent you brought into this house has disappeared, too. I don't know what kinds of people you ordinarily associate with, Gannon," he sneered. "But the Wildings aren't accustomed to having criminals as house guests."

"Marshall." The word was a warning, and came from Red.

"You should have listened to me last night, Father, and gotten rid of him there and then." The color in Marshall's face was dangerously high.

Richard's gaze automatically went to Slade for a more rational explanation.

"It's my fault, Gannon. Marsh came over to see if the boys were here. I heard him shouting at Dad and left Jay alone upstairs while I tried to find out what was going on. When I came back, he was gone. I think he must have overheard, and Marshall said some pretty harsh things. I'm sorry."

"And Chip and Wally? Does anyone know where they are?"

Marshall interjected. "They left home this morning after I expressly told them to stay away from that little con artist. I haven't seen my boys since. He's probably got them somewhere. Regina's hysterical."

She would be, thought Lauren cynically. "How could he have taken them anywhere? He's been with Slade all day."

In a calm voice Richard asked, "What time did you get back here, Slade?"

"Not more than an hour ago. Jay was . . . mellow, Gannon. He seemed to enjoy the stables." He turned to his brother. "Wouldn't a more rational explanation be that he heard you say they were missing and went to look for them?"

"Him?" The word, as Marshall delivered it, was an insult. "I can't imagine a Philly street kid as a Good Samaritan."

"Marshall Wilding, you are the slimiest . . ." Richard's voice was low and dangerous. "Is there not a bone of compassion in your body?"

Marshall was almost apoplectic. "Now look here, Gannon . . ."

"For your information, I'm a Philly street kid." He poked his own chest, looking like some little boy bent on a scrap.

Lauren interrupted them. "Shut up, all of you. Jay can't have been gone long. We don't even know if he's with the boys. But the important thing now is to get all of them back to the house before dark. You can hurl insults at each other later."

Marshall looked as if he might argue, but Slade and Richard immediately agreed.

"Slade, you and your father know the area best. Tell us where to go." Richard included both of them in his request.

Red deferred to his son. "Slade rides the land on horseback. He knows the country better than I."

Slade thought for a minute. "I'll take a horse and search around the lake. Marshall, you can go with me. Richard, you search those dense woods on the east side of the property. You'll have to go on foot. Be careful. That area's full of snakes."

Silence followed his words as the possibilities dawned. Marshall, Slade and Lauren had grown up playing in these woods. Chip and Wally, too, knew to be cautious. Jay might be a streetwise kid, but here in the country he was the greenest kind of tenderfoot.

"I'll go with Richard," offered Red.

"Dad," said Slade carefully. "We need someone to stay by the base station."

"Oh, all right," he grumbled. "You just think I'm too old."

"What about me?"

The men looked at Lauren blankly. Marshall cleared his throat. "You stay here, Lauren," he instructed, trying to regain his lost authority as the eldest.

She looked at him, her blue eyes full of amusement and derision. "Don't be an ass, Marshall."

"You take the Jeep, Lauren," Slade instructed. "Try to cover the back roads between here and the highway. The radio's working, isn't it?"

Lauren was already heading for her father's study to get the portable transmitters, so Red answered for her. "Have you ever known me not to keep the radio in perfect working order?" he asked rather huffily.

In seconds Lauren was back. She handed out the walkie-talkies and started for the door.

Richard stopped her for a minute with a hand on her arm. "Everyone check in with Red on the half-hour. Is that okay?" He glanced at Red, received a nod. "Be careful, honey," he said to Lauren.

She gave him a quick kiss. "You, too, Gannon. Watch out for snakes."

Red had a parting shot for them all. "For crying out loud, find them before this damn party starts!"

SOME OF THE ROADS hadn't been tended to in years, but blessedly the old Jeep made up in dependability for what it lacked in beauty. Lauren tried to picture the aerial photograph of the property that hung in the study. Which road would the boys be likely to try? Or Jay? Despite everything, her heart ached for the boy, who must have overheard Marshall's harsh judgement. Damn Marshall! Why did he have to be such a stiff-necked prig? None of the rest of them was that way. At least she hoped *she* wasn't. She hoped she had a bigger heart. So far, though, there wasn't much evidence to prove she did.

She hadn't been willing to work with Richard in trying to help Jay. And surely it was just as bad to wash your hands of a problem, to walk away from it, as it was to blame it on someone else. Burdens were easier to shoulder if they were shared, and she had refused to share Richard's burden. Well, she hadn't exactly refused, but she hadn't offered an alternative plan, either.

The Jeep hit a rock, and she bounced so hard her crown made contact with the roof. "Ouch!" Bringing the vehicle to a stop, she squeezed her eyes shut and rubbed the top of her head.

After checking in with her father, she replaced the microphone on its metal hook. Still no word. She sighed. She was about to put the Jeep in gear again, when she heard a noise that hadn't been audible over the squawk of the radio or the noise of the active engine.

Switching off the motor, she cocked her head to one side, then the other, trying to pinpoint the source of the rustling murmuring sound. It seemed to be coming from the copse of pines above the road.

She stepped out of the Jeep and looked up. What she saw caused her heart to thump violently in her breast. Smoke curled skyward. "Oh, no," she breathed. Her sneakers gave her purchase as she scrambled up the bank and into the woods. She made her way through the dense undergrowth, oblivious to the vines that clawed at her clothes and occasionally her skin. Gradually she became aware of another sound—an angry voice. But it wasn't truly angry...it was more frantic. As she broke through to the clearing the scene that met her eyes made her want to both laugh and cry.

The fire was not dangerous at this point, but left unattended, it would become so in a very short time. The two Wilding boys were standing helplessly aside while Jay fought the flames alone. He was stomping the creeping embers as they spread across the grassy clearing.

"We can help," shouted Chip.

"I started it! Why won't you let me help?" wailed Wally.

"Because if you got scorched your father would see my hide strung up on the closest oak tree, that's why. Mustn't singe the delicate skin of a Wilding," he sneered.

Beneath the bravado, Lauren could hear the fright and panic in his voice. He pulled off his shirt to swat ineffectually at the growing flames with it.

"You're a dumb little jerk, Wally Wilding, and if you don't watch yourself you're going to end up a punk just like me, always in trouble, always—" Whatever else he'd been about to say was choked off by a sob he tried to camouflage as a cough.

"Are you crying, Jay?" Wally asked, unbelieving.

Jay whirled on him. "No, I . . ." His words died in his throat when he saw Lauren standing behind them. His eyes grew large in his smoke-blackened, tear-streaked face; his adolescent Adam's apple bobbled in his throat.

She kept her gaze on him, but spoke to her nephews. "Chip, Wally, the Jeep is down on the road. There's a tarp and a blanket in the back. Go get them. Use the radio to tell the others where we are."

"Aunt Lauren, we—"

"Now," she ordered. They went crashing through the underbrush in the direction from which she'd come.

Her next movement was completely spontaneous. She couldn't have said later what motivated her to walk forward and put her arms around the slight body of the boy. She gave a fleeting thought to the fire, but the way she felt right now, the whole forest could have burned—this was more important.

His shoulder muscles bunched, preparing to resist the embrace. His arms hung lifelessly at his sides. She simply held him tighter.

"Oh, God," he said, holding his breath, fighting the break that was coming. "Oh, God," he repeated with a shudder. "I'm sorry. I'm so sorry. Those kids are.... I wouldn't hurt them for anything." The sob that burst forth came from deep within him, from a place so deep and so tormented Lauren couldn't even imagine the extent of his pain and anguish.

She wrapped her arms as tightly as she could, rocking him slightly. "Let it out, Jay. It will help to let it out. I promise."

He tried again. "The fire . . ."

"To hell with the fire. You're more important."

His arms came around her waist, his fists clinging to her blouse as he sagged against her. The mournful lament that shook his frail body so violently should never be endured by any human being, much less a child, Lauren thought.

She was crying, too. For Jay, for Richard, for herself.

Finally one last shuddering sob shook him, and he straightened his shoulders, pulling away. When he saw the tears that streaked her face he stiffened with shock. He put out a hand to touch her arm. It was a telling gesture, that reaching out to another person. She doubted that he'd ever done that, except maybe to Richard.

"Please don't cry, Miss Wilding," he pleaded, wiping his own tears away on his bare forearm. "I've been . . ." He sighed, a very adult sound. "You know, Gannon is the only one who's ever been decent to me. I guess I thought . . ."

"I know what you thought, Jay. You thought I would squeeze you out. I'm sorry, too." She gave a broken laugh and reached out to smooth back a lock of dark hair that had fallen forward over his brow. "I'm supposed to be the grown-up around here, but I acted pretty childishly."

They heard the boys approaching. The business of putting out the fire had to be addressed. "We'll talk later, okay?"

"Thank you." His wavering smile and husky voice brought the tears to her eyes again.

She cleared her throat. "How did the fire start, anyway?"

"Cigars," he admitted quietly.

Actually, Jay had done a good job of containing the flames on the side where they might have found their way into the thick, dry undergrowth. Only the grass in the clearing still burned. They stamped and swatted until every smoldering ember had been extinguished. By the time they'd finished they all looked like things the proverbial cat wouldn't have bothered with.

Lauren looked at Jay; Wally looked at Lauren and Chip. Then Jay shook his head at the sight of the begrimed boys and laughed. It was a strange sound, stiff, as though he didn't do it often. With unspoken intuition they all came together in a four-way hug, laughing in relief, patting one another on their backs in congratulation.

When the men found them a few minutes later they were lying on their backs in the charred grass, resting from the exertion of battling the fire. They were still chuckling.

Richard was the first one through the brush. He didn't hear their soft laughter. He froze, squeezing his eyes shut to deny the scene.

"Oh, Lord!" said Marshall, coming up behind him.

Like a flash of lightning, before anyone could make a move, Lauren was on her feet between her brother and the boys.

Richard's jaw dropped in astonishment.

She planted her hands on her hips, thrust her chin obstinately. "Don't you dare say a word, Marshall," she spat, like a jungle cat ready to protect her young, completely forgetting that two of the young were, in fact, his. "Not one word! This whole thing is your fault. You should have shown a little understanding to Jay as a friend of Wally's and Chip's. But if someone doesn't fit into what you consider to be the proper mold, you brush him off as if he were an annoying fly. I don't know how you developed that attitude. Mother and Daddy certainly didn't encourage us to think that way."

Marshall was pale. He had stood perfectly still under her tirade. "No, they didn't," he said quietly.

"You should be apologizing to these boys," she ranted on.

He looked steadily beyond her shoulder at the three faces that reflected a dawning comprehension so far lost on Lauren in her anger. "Lauren's right. When I thought that any one of you might be in danger, I realized that the blame was mostly mine. I'm really sorry, boys." His sincerity was clear to the youngsters, and to Richard. "I hope you can forgive me."

Lauren, deaf to his apology, opened her mouth. Richard intervened before she could say any more. "Slow down, wildcat," he murmured, pulling her under his arm. "You made your point."

Wally and Chip rushed straight to their father when he opened his arms. Marshall's eyes, however, remained on Jay. "I hope you can forgive me, too, Jay."

Looking at the ground, Jay shuffled his feet, self-conscious now that the emotional danger was over.

Richard spoke softly. "Jay?"

Their eyes met. Jay nodded, understanding.

Richard's own eyes narrowed speculatively. Something colored the boy's expression that had never been there before. The anger was gone. In its place Richard saw a kind of tranquillity coupled with a grim determination. He sighed in overwhelming relief, recognizing the signs, at last, that Jay had made some sort of a breakthrough.

Jay turned to Marshall. "It's all right, Mr. Wilding. I was acting like a horse's a—"

Suddenly he was all embarrassed, a state so uncommon to Jay that Lauren wanted to laugh out loud. Though she suspected he would probably revert to his belligerent pose from time to time, she sincerely hoped it would not happen frequently. But when he did it wouldn't matter. She had broken through the protective wall once; she could do it again. She felt Richard sag slightly in relief.

His smile, when it met hers, was full of hope. "I don't know what the hell happened here, but I'm grateful."

"You might say Jay and I both learned a lesson."

"I learned one, too," he said, sober again. "When I walked out of the woods and saw you lying there . . . For just a second before you moved, I thought something had happened to you. God! I wanted to die!" His arm tightened. He buried his face in her hair and took a long shuddering breath, remembering. "Lauren, no matter how, on any terms, we have to be together. I love you so much."

She wrapped her arms around his waist, holding him as she'd held Jay. "Where's the ring?"

He raised his head. His sexy smile turned her knees to jelly. "In my pocket. You want it now?"

"In a minute."

"You want to show it off at the party?"

"Good Lord, I'd forgotten the party. Look at us. Jay, we have to hurry and get cleaned up."

"Your mother won't be mad, will she?" the boy asked.

"No, she won't be mad at all. She'll be so relieved that we're all right." She tilted her head back to grin up at Richard. "We're going to be all right, aren't we? All three of us," she said, happiness shining out of her eyes.

One hand slid up under her hair to circle her neck. The look he gave her was so filled with love and tenderness it sent her heart straight up to fill her throat. "We're going to be better than all right," he murmured. "We're going to be fantastic. All four or five or six of us."

"Gannon! Four, five maybe, but six?" Her voice rose on the last word. Jay laughed, and she glared at him.

Richard chuckled exultantly. "Maybe even seven . . . or eight. We can afford them—we're rich!"

"Yes, darling. We're very, very rich." They both knew that she wasn't talking about money.

Harlequin Temptation

COMING NEXT MONTH

#117 A PERMANENT ARRANGEMENT
Jane Silverwood

Ben Gallagher brought new meaning to the words "love thy neighbor." One week after moving in across the street, the sexy bachelor was making moves on Paula.

#118 DIAMOND IN THE ROUGH
Helen Conrad

Cal James was just the man Marlo Santee needed for her latest ad campaign. And she knew just the way to rope him into doing it!

#119 SERENDIPITY Judith McWilliams

What does the theft of a small white mouse have to do with a famous research scientist pursuing one of the cleaning staff? Find out in the madcap yet steamy romantic romp of Ann and Marcus.

#120 BY INVITATION ONLY
Lorena McCourtney

Most reluctantly Shar agreed to test the fidelity of her best friend's man . . . via seduction. But when she discovered she wanted Tal O'Neil all to herself, her loyalty was on the line. . . .

WIN GREAT PRIZES
Claim Lots of Free Gifts

If you missed our ad in the center section of this novel, use the coupon below.

We'll send you lots of free gifts just for trying our Reader Service…4 full-length current stories of love and romance, an elegant velveteen jewelry bag, and a surprise free gift, one that will really delight you.

FREE gifts!

AND we'll also automatically qualify you for all featured prizes in our Super Celebration Sweepstakes…prizes like A Dozen Roses + a Dozen Crisp $100 bills—birthstone earrings—your choice of a stunning Mink or Fox Jacket—mounds of delicious Godiva Chocolates—an Island-in-the-Sun vacation for 2—and Perfume Collections direct from France.

FREE prizes!

There is no catch, no obligation when you say YES to all this. We'll simply send you collections of our newest and best love stories every month or so…AND YOU DECIDE. Keep what you like at big discounts off store prices, with free home delivery in the bargain. Return all others postpaid. Even quit the Service anytime, no questions asked.

BIG SAVINGS!

All gifts and prizes you win are yours no matter what. Simply fill in Coupon below, clip and mail—TODAY!

- -

MAIL TO **Harlequin Reader Service**

IN U.S.A.: 901 Fuhrmann Blvd. Box #1867, Buffalo NY 14240
IN CANADA: Box #2800, 5170 Yonge St. Postal Station A Willowdale, Ontario M3N 6J3

YES, I'll try the Harlequin Reader Service under the terms specified above. Send me 4 FREE BOOKS and all other FREE GIFTS. I understand that I also automatically qualify for ALL Super Celebration prizes and prize features advertised in 1986.

BIRTHDAY INFORMATION		

NAME _____

MONTH _____

ADDRESS _____ APT # _____

DAY _____
We'll tell you on your birthday what you win.

CITY _____ STATE/PROV. ____ ZIP/POST CODE ____

Gift offer limited to new subscribers, 1 per household & terms & prices subject to change. No purchase necessary. Check this box ☐ if you only want to enter Sweeps for single set of prizes—fur jacket and candies.

SWT

═══ OFFICIAL RULES ═══

Harlequin "Super Celebration"
SWEEPSTAKES

NEW PRIZES—NEW PRIZE FEATURES & CHOICES—MONTHLY

1. To enter the sweepstakes, follow the instructions outlined on the Center Insert Card. Alternate means of entry, NO PURCHASE NECESSARY, you may also enter by mailing your name, address and birthday on a plain 3″ x 5″ piece of paper to: In U.S.A.: Harlequin "Super Celebration" Sweepstakes, P.O. Box 1867, Buffalo, N.Y. 14240-1867. In Canada: Harlequin "Super Celebration" Sweepstakes, P.O. Box 2800, 5170 Yonge Street, Postal Station A, Willowdale, Ontario M2N 6J3.

2. Winners will be selected in random drawings from all entries received. All prizes will be awarded. These prizes are in addition to any free gifts which might be offered. Versions of this sweepstakes with different prizes may appear in other presentations by TorStar and their affiliates. The maximum value of the prizes offered is $8,000.00. Winners selected will receive the prize offered from their prize package.

3. The selection of winners will be conducted under the supervision of Marden-Kane, an independent judging organization. By entering the sweepstakes, each entrant accepts and agrees to be bound by these rules and the decision of the judges which shall be final and binding. Odds of winning are dependent upon the total number of entries received. Taxes, if any, are the sole responsibility of the winners. Prizes are not transferable. This sweepstakes is scheduled to appear in Retail Outlets of Harlequin Books during the period of June 1986 to December 1986. All entries must be received by January 31st, 1987. The drawing will take place on or about March 1st, 1987 at the offices of Marden-Kane, Lake Success, New York. For Quebec (Canada) residents, any litigation regarding the running of this sweepstakes and the awarding of prizes must be submitted to La Regie de Lotteries et Course du Quebec.

4. This presentation offers the prizes as illustrated on the Center Insert Card.

5. This offer is open to residents of the U.S., and Canada, 18 years or older, except employees of TorStar, its affilliates, subsidiaries, Marden-Kane and all other agencies and persons connected with conducting this sweepstakes. All Federal, State and local laws apply. Void where prohibited or restricted by law. Winners will be notified by mail and may be required to execute an affidavit of eligibility and release which must be returned within 14 days after notification. Winners consent to the use of their name, photograph and/or likeness for advertising and publicity in conjunction with this and similar promotions without additional compensation. One prize per family or household. Canadian winners will be required to answer a skill testing question.

6. For a list of our most recent prize winners, send a stamped, self-addressed envelope to: WINNERS LIST, c/o Marden-Kane, P.O. Box 525, Sayreville, NJ 08872.

No Lucky Number needed to win!

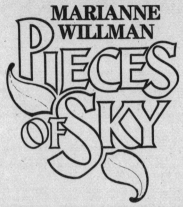
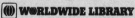

HARLEQUIN HISTORICAL

Explore love with Harlequin in the Middle Ages, the Renaissance, in the Regency, the Victorian and other eras.

Relive within these books the endless ages of romance, set against authentic historical backgrounds. Two new historical love stories published each month.

*Shay Flanagan is Gypsy,
the raven-haired beauty who inflamed passion
in the hearts of two Falconer men.*

Carole Mortimer

GYPSY

Lyon Falconer, a law unto himself, claimed Shay—when he didn't have the right. Ricky Falconer, gentle and loving married Shay—when she had no other choice.

Now her husband's death brings Shay back within Lyon's grasp. Once and for all Lyon intends to prove that Shay has always been—will always be—*his* Gypsy!

Published by MQ Publications Limited
12 The Ivories, 6–8 Northampton Street
London N1 2HY
Tel: 020 7359 2244
Fax: 020 7359 1616
email: mail@mqpublications.com

With special thanks to The International Shakespeare Globe Centre
Limited for their help with this project, particularly
Jane Arrowsmith and Nicholas Robins.

Plans for the new Globe © Pentagram Design Limited.
Illustration of the Swan theatre on page 158 reproduced by
permission of the Department of Manuscripts at the University of Utrecht.

Every effort has been made to trace copyright holders and
MQ Publications apologise for any unintentional omissions.
We would be pleased to insert acknowledgments as
appropriate in any further edition of this publication.

ISBN: 1 84072 038 7

4 6 8 9 7 5 3

Printed and bound in China

a little brown notebook

Shakespeare
at the Globe

David Baird

MQP

Contents

– Shakespeare at the Globe –

Imagine a place unlike any other. A place dedicated to the study, appreciation and excellence in performance of great plays. Imagine that place as a faithful reconstruction of an Elizabethan theatre situated close to the banks of London's famous River Thames. Imagine all this, and you'll find yourself at the entrance to theatre's greatest gift – Shakespeare's Globe.

It would be impossible to write anything concerning Shakespeare's Globe without first paying tribute to another extraordinary man – Sam Wanamaker (1919-1993), a talented American actor, whose vision and tenacity has given us one of the most remarkable theatres in existence today. The Globe provides us with both a valuable insight into theatre during the Elizabethan period *and* a unique opportunity to experience for ourselves how Shakespeare's plays are most likely to have appeared on stage.

below: view of London's theatres from an early seventeenth-century
engraving by Cornelius Visscher.

Shakespeare's London

All the world's a stage,
And all the men and women merely players...

As You Like It, Act II, sc vii

– Shakespeare at the Globe –

The original Globe was built in London in 1599, at a time when the city was undergoing major changes. The second half of the sixteenth century saw the restoration of Protestantism after the brief but austere reign of the Catholic Queen Mary I, during which heresy trials, denunciations, persecutions and burnings were familiar elements of London life. With the coronation of Elizabeth I in 1558 a new era of toleration was ushered in along with a revival of interest in learning and new ideas. Explorers such as Sir Francis Drake and Sir Walter Raleigh were returning with exciting tales of other lands, and London felt itself to be the hub of excitement.

This royal throne of kings, this scept'red isle,
This earth of majesty, this seat of Mars,
This other Eden, demi-paradise,
This fortress built by Nature for herself
Against infection and the hand of war,
This happy breed of men, this little world,
This precious stone set in the silver sea,
Which serves it in the office of a wall,
Or as a moat defensive to a house,
Against the envy of less happier lands;
This blessed plot, this earth, this realm,
    this England...

Richard II, Act II, sc i

Shakespeare's London was a bustling centre of business, its population had more than doubled in the last half of the sixteenth century, making it the biggest city in Europe. Situated on the banks of the River Thames, London was perfectly placed to capitalise on growing trade opportunities. Numerous new London trading enterprises such as the Russia Company, the Levant Company and the East India Company were set up, and it was possible for merchants to make huge fortunes. The wealth generated by the City acted as a magnet and the population continued to grow as migrants were attracted not only from the rest of England but from all over Europe.

right: detail from a map of London by
Braun and Hohenburg, 1572.

For much of Shakespeare's life, England was ruled by Queen Elizabeth I. She was a remarkable woman who, despite great odds and with exceptional determination, vision and wisdom, saw to it that England enjoyed 45 years of peace and prosperity. Born in 1533, Elizabeth I was the daughter of King Henry VIII and Anne Boleyn. When she was only three years old her mother was executed for treason. During 1554 the Princess Elizabeth was imprisoned in the Tower of London by her Catholic half-sister Queen Mary. Four years later, after Mary's death in 1558, Elizabeth was crowned Queen.

left: woodcut of Elizabeth I.

– Notes –

What was it actually like to experience Shakespeare's London first hand? An account noted during a visit by Frederick Duke of Wurtemberg in 1592 gives a fascinating picture of what it must have been like to walk through the overcrowded streets.

London is a large, excellent and mighty city of business, and the most important in the whole kingdom; most of the inhabitants are employed in buying and selling merchandise, and trading in almost every corner of the world...

It is a very populous city, so that one can scarcely pass along the streets, on account of the throng.

The inhabitants are magnificently apparelled, and are extremely proud and overbearing; and because the greater part, especially the trades-people, seldom go into other countries, but always remain in their houses in the city attending to their business, they care little for foreigners, but scoff and laugh at them; and moreover one dare not oppose them, else the street-boys and apprentices collect together in immense crowds and strike to the right and left unmercifully without regard to person; and because they are the strongest, one is obliged to put up with the insult as well as the injury. The women have much more liberty than perhaps in any other place; they also know well how to make use of it, for they go dressed out in exceedingly fine clothes, and give all their attention to their ruffs and stuffs, to such a degree indeed, that, as I am informed, many a one does not hesitate to wear velvet in the streets, which is common with them, whilst at home perhaps they have not a piece of dry bread...

The crowded streets of London may have been vital and bustling during the day, but Shakespeare describes a gloomy and treacherous picture of London by night...

> *when the searching eye of heaven is hid*
> *Behind the globe, and lights the lower world,*
> *Then thieves and robbers range abroad unseen,*
> *In murders, and in outrage bloody here.*

> *Richard II*, Act III, sc ii

– *Notes* –

– *Notes* –

– Notes –

– *Notes* –

In an overcrowded city like Elizabethan London, any activity that drew crowds was a potential threat to public order. The Lord Mayors of the City, nervous that the large numbers of people attracted by plays would cause a public nuisance, tried to get them banned for much of Elizabeth's reign. It was believed that plays distracted apprentices and workmen from their jobs, and that the crowded theatres were a breeding ground for the plague which periodically broke out in the City, especially during the summer months.

Concerns about the theatres as a danger to morality and health were voiced in a letter from Bishop Grindal of London to Sir William Cecil in 1564.

> Mr Calfhill this morning showed me your letter
> to him, wherein ye wish some politic orders
> to be devised against infection. I think it very
> necessary... there is no one thing of late is more
> like to have renewed this contagion than the
> practice of an idle sort of people which have been
> infamous in all commonweals: I mean these
> histriones, common players, who now daily, but
> specially on holidays, set up bills, whereunto the
> youth restoreth excessively and there taketh
> infection: besides that God's word by their
> impure mouths is profaned and turned into
> scoffs. For remedy whereof in my judgement,
> ye should do very well to... inhibit all plays for
> one whole year (and if it were for ever it were
> not amiss) within the City of three miles'
> compass...

– *Notes* –

– *Notes* –

Fear of the plague was immense, as is suggested by the lengths to which people went to try and protect themselves from it. Here is a 'Treatment for the Plague' published in *The English Hus-wife*, 1615, by Gervase Markham.

> *To preserve your body from the infection of the*
> *plague, you shall take a quart of old ale, and*
> *after it hath risen upon the fire and hath*
> *been scummed, you shall put there-into of*
> *aristolochialonga, of angelica and of celandine of*
> *each half an handful, and boil them well therein;*
> *then strain the drink through a clean cloth, and*
> *dissolve therein a drachm of the best mithridate,*
> *as much ivory finely powdered and searched,*
> *and six spoonful of dragon-water, then put it*
> *in a close glass: and every morning fasting take*
> *five spoonful thereof, and after bite and chew*
> *in your mouth the dried root of angelica, or*
> *smell, as on a nose-gay, to the tassled-end of a*
> *ship rope, and they will surely preserve you*
> *from infection.*

The straight-laced Puritans wanted to see plays banned. They believed that the theatre encouraged profane and ungodly behaviour, and that the plague was a judgement from God.

Look but upon the common plays in London, and see the multitude that flocketh to them and followeth them. Behold the sumptuous theatre houses, a continual monument of London's prodigality and folly. But I understand they are now forbidden because of the plague. I like the policy well if it hold still, for a disease is but lodged or patched up that is not cured in the cause, and the cause of plagues is sin, if you look to it well: and the cause of sin are plays: therefore the cause of plagues are plays.

Thomas White, *A Sermon Preached at Paules Crosse 1578*

Will not a filthy play, with the blast of a
trumpet, sooner call thither a thousand, than an
hour's tolling of a bell bring to the sermon a
hundred?

> John Stockwood, *A Sermon Preached at
> Paules Crosse 1578*

The writers of our time are so led away with
vainglory, that their only endeavour is to
pleasure the humour of men...

> *A Second and Third Blast of Retrait from
> Plaies and Theatres 1580*

– Notes –

The City authorities were keen to discredit the theatres and sought for any reason to close them to the public. Lord Mayor Blank wrote the following letter to Lord Burghley on January 14th 1583 after an unfortunate accident at Paris Garden in Southwark.

It may please your Lordship to be further advertised (which I think you have already heard) of a great mishap at Paris Garden, where by ruin of all the scaffolds at once yesterday, a great number of people are some presently slain and some maimed and grievously hurt. It giveth great occasion to acknowledge the hand of God for such abuse of the Sabbath day, and moveth me in conscience to beseech your lordship to give order for redress of such contempt of God's service.

– Notes –

If it were not for the protection of the Royal Court, Elizabethan drama would probably have come to an end under unceasing pressure from the City authorities and the Puritans before Shakespeare even arrived in London. But Elizabeth I loved being entertained, and her Privy Council protected the theatres on the grounds that they supplied well-practised and professional players to perform the plays that the Queen enjoyed.

> *Come now; what masques, what dances*
>   *shall we have,*
> *To wear away this long age of three hours*
> *Between our after-supper and bed-time?*
> *Where is our usual manager of mirth?*
> *What revels are in hand? Is there no play*
> *To ease the anguish of a torturing hour?*

> *A Midsummer Night's Dream*, Act V, sc i

right: an Elizabethan masque.

One school of thought is that Elizabeth inherited the thriftiness of her grandfather, Henry VII, and intentionally set out to get her entertainment as cheaply as possible. By encouraging London's public theatres she was establishing somewhere for players to practise, other than at her Court's expense. A Master of Revelry would have been appointed at Court, under the charge of the Lord Chamberlain, and it was his job to invite acting companies to submit plays for selection. The character of Philostrate in *A Midsummer Night's Dream* plays just such a role, selecting plays to be performed before the Duke of Athens, Theseus...

A play there is, my lord, some ten words long,
Which is as brief as I have known a play.
But by ten words, my lord, it is too long,
Which makes it tedious; for in all the play
There is not one word apt, one player fitted.
And tragical, my noble lord, it is,
For Pyramus therein doth kill himself.
Which when I saw rehearsed, I must confess,
Made mine eyes water; but more merry tears
The passion of loud laughter never shed.

A Midsummer Night's Dream, Act V, sc i

In 1594 the Lord Mayor of London and the Lord Chamberlain (the Queen's Privy Councillor in charge of plays) reached an agreement about the future of the theatre in the City. Only two companies of players were permitted to perform within the City or suburbs. One of these companies was the Lord Chamberlain's Men, to which Shakespeare belonged. This group occupied the Theatre in Shoreditch to the north of the City. The other company was the Lord Admiral's Men, who occupied the Rose on the south bank of the Thames, and numbered the brilliant young poet and playwright Christopher Marlowe among its members.

– Notes –

Here, the Lord Chamberlain (Lord Hunsdon) puts his case to Lord Mayor Martin, on October 8th 1594, promising that his players will conduct themselves in a restrained and respectable manner...

Where now my company of players have been accustomed for the better exercise of their quality and for the service of her Majesty if need so require, to play this winter time within the City at the Cross Keys in Gracechurch Street, these are to require and pray your Lordship... to permit and suffer them so to do... they have undertaken to me that, where heretofore they begin not their plays till towards four o'clock, they will now begin at two and have done between four and five, and will not use any drums or trumpets at all for the calling of people together, and shall be contributories to the poor of the parish where they play, according to their abilities.

right: William Kemp, dancer and comedian with the Lord Chamberlain's Men until 1599.

If we shadows have offended,
Think but this, and all is mended,:
That you have but slumb'red here,
While these visions did appear.
And this weak and idle theme,
No more yielding but a dream...

A Midsummer Night's Dream, Act V, sc i

– Notes –

– Notes –

With only two companies of players permitted to perform within the City or suburbs, and with these remaining playhouses regularly closed down during the summer months due to the plague, it was not only the play-going public who suffered. It also came as a shock to the pockets of the watermen of the Thames, who had a lucrative trade in ferrying theatre-goers back and forth across the river. Here they petition Lord Admiral Howard, outlining their plight, following the closure of the Rose during an outbreak of plague...

right: Thames waterman.

Whereas your good Lordship had directed your warrant unto her majesty's Justices for the restraint of a playhouse belonging unto the said Philip Henslowe, one of the grooms of her Majesty's Chamber, so it is, if it please your good Lordship, that we your said poor watermen have had much help and relief for us our poor wives and children by means of the resort of such people as come unto the said playhouse. It may therefore please your good lordship for God's sake and in the way of charity to respect us your poor watermen, and to give leave unto the said Philip Henslowe to have playing in his said house during such time as others have, according as it hath been accustomed.

The Court of Elizabeth I was a vibrant centre for poets, musicians, writers and players. The Queen, however, was fonder of music and dancing than she was of poetry and drama. The competition for royal patronage with great composers such as Thomas Campion, William Byrd and Orlando Gibbons, influenced the development of drama. Consequently many of the plays of Shakespeare and his contemporaries contain songs and even ballets.

The play *Twelfth Night*, written between 1601 and 1602 would have been performed before the Queen at Court. Its final scene closes with the Clown's song;

> When that I was and a little tiny boy,
> With hey, ho, the wind and the rain,
> A foolish thing was but a toy,
> For the rain it raineth every day...
>
> A great while ago the world begun
> With hey, ho, the wind and the rain,
> But that's all one, our play is done,
> And we'll strive to please you every day.

Twelfth Night, Act V, sc i

left: seventeenth-century woodcut of a musician.

– Notes –

The theatre wasn't the only amusement available in Elizabethan London: bear-baiting was a far older form of entertainment which enjoyed the patronage of both Queen Elizabeth I and King James I. The sport took place in special arenas, one of which, the Bear Garden, was situated very close to the original Globe and catered for the same audience. One theatre proprietor, Philip Henslowe, even made sure that the playhouse he was building in 1613 was capable of staging both activities.

The character Sir Andrew Aguecheek in *Twelfth Night* bewails his misspent youth, with too much time squandered on the popular pastimes of the period...

> *I would I had bestowed that time in the tongues*
> *that I have in fencing, dancing and bear-baiting.*
> *O, had I but followed the arts!*

Twelfth Night, Act I, sc iii

– *Notes* –

A German traveller, Lupold von Wedel, visited Southwark in 1584 and recorded his experience of bear-baiting. He described a round building three storeys high where about a hundred large English dogs were kept in separate wooden kennels. The dogs fought individually with three bears, the second larger than the first, and the third larger than the second. After that a horse was brought in and chased by the dogs, then a bull who 'defended himself bravely'. Further revelry was had when a number of men and women came forward from a separate compartment and danced, fought and conversed with each other, while another man threw white bread into the audience, who scrambled for it. Von Wedel described a rose overhead in the middle of the structure which, being set alight by a rocket, released hundreds of apples and pears onto the audience. While they chased for these more rockets and fireworks were set off among the crowd, marking the end of the entertainment!

right: seventeenth-century woodcut showing bear-baiting at a German theatre.

Thomas Platter, visiting London from Basle in Switzerland in 1599, experienced plays at both the newly built Globe and later at the Curtain in Shoreditch where he says, 'At the end they danced very elegantly both in English and in Irish fashion.'

He capers, he dances, he has eyes of youth, he writes verses, he speaks holiday, he smells April and May.

The Merry Wives of Windsor, Act III, sc ii

– Notes –

– Notes –

The
First Globe

*...and here's a marvellous convenient place for our rehearsal.
This green plot shall be our stage, this hawthorn brake our
tiring-house; and we will do it in action, as we will do it
before the Duke.*

A Midsummer Night's Dream, Act III, sc i

The Globe didn't begin life as the Globe, when actor/manager James Burbage erected his playhouse in 1576 he chose to call it the 'Theatre'. This established the name by which playhouses (as the Elizabethans called them) were to be known by future generations.

– Notes –

When James Burbage built the Theatre he cleverly found a plot of land in Shoreditch, on a busy road going north out of the City. This placed it just outside the jurisdiction of the play-hating Lord Mayors: all areas of London within the City walls, except for the cathedral precincts, Blackfriars and Southwark, came under their control.

right: map of London in Shakespeare's time, showing the city walls and the position of the theatres.

– The First Globe –

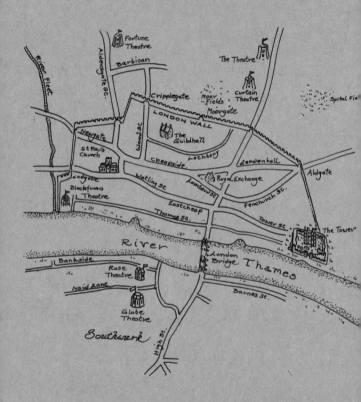

In 1596 James Burbage attempted to renew his lease on the Theatre, but the landlord, Mr Giles Allen, refused. Burbage was compelled to look for another venue for his company of players. Eventually he bought the habitable ruins of Blackfriars Priory, just below St. Pauls in the City, where he built a private theatre. Here he struck a problem: the local inhabitants petitioned against it on the grounds of noise and plague. Their appeal succeeded and Lord Cobham, the Lord Chamberlain, refused to let the theatre open.

In an effort to minimise his losses, James Burbage sub-let the theatre to a group of child actors who, it seems, were less offensive to the residents of Blackfriars. In *Hamlet* Shakespeare refers to the fashion for such infant actors...

> *...an aery of children, little eyases, that cry out*
> *on the top of question, and are most tyrannically*
> *clapp'd for 't.*
>
> *Hamlet,* Act II, sc ii

right: St.Pauls, before the Great Fire of 1666.

– Notes –

– Notes –

– Notes –

James Burbage died early in 1597, leaving his sons Cuthbert and Richard to try to save the situation. While the battle to renew the lease on the Theatre went on, the company of players continued to perform in a rented playhouse called the Curtain. Towards the very end of 1598 they managed to lease a plot of land only a short distance from the Rose theatre on the south bank of the River Thames. If they couldn't persuade Giles Allen to renew the lease on the Theatre in Shoreditch, then they would use a lateral approach. Employing a master carpenter named Peter Street, they disassembled the Theatre and arranged for it to be floated across the river to the new site. Here it was rebuilt with the new name of the Globe.

The Globe took its name from its sign which pictured Hercules. A flag showing Hercules carrying the world on his shoulders flew above the theatre whenever a play was in progress.

– Notes –

Following their legal wrangles, the Burbage brothers could no longer afford to pay for the rebuilding of their playhouse. As a way of raising funds they offered their four leading players shares in the building – and so William Shakespeare came to be the owner of one-eighth of the Globe.

– *Notes* –

– Notes –

– Notes –

– Notes –

The main competition to the Globe came from its neighbour the Rose. This playhouse, the first to be constructed on the south bank of the Thames, was built in the 1580s by a dyer, theatrical lessee and speculator by the name of Philip Henslowe.

A Dutchman, by the name of De Witt, visiting London around 1596 [before the Globe was built] made the following comments about its playhouses...

> There are four amphitheatres in London of notable beauty... In each of them a different play is daily exhibited to the populace. The two more magnificent of these are situated to the south beyond the Thames and are called the Rose and the Swan.

– Notes –

Philip Henslowe, proprietor of the Rose, acted as a kind of play broker. He would buy plays and then sell them on, finding a profit for himself in the middle. Entries in his diary include the purchase of a velvet cloak for £16 and £4.14s for hose, yet the highest price he paid for a play before 1600 was only £8 (£4 for the cheapest). The price rose after 1600 to £20 for a play by a writer of good repute.

The Elizabethan appetite for theatre must have been enormous. It is recorded that in February 1592, following a major rebuilding of the Rose, there was room for a 25 per cent increase in the number of groundlings (those members of the audience who crammed the floor space around the stage). In that month, their first in season, Lord Strange's Men and their star actor Edward Alleyn performed 105 performances of 23 plays in only 19 weeks! Lord Strange's men continued their residence at the Rose for two years. The Rose continued to flourish with many good crowd-drawing companies, such as the Lord Admiral's Men, who were in residence until 1599.

– Notes –

– Notes –

– Notes –

– Notes –

Philip Henslowe understood theatre and audiences, and his seasons at the Rose were extremely popular. There are also suggestions that troupes of players were out touring in the country under his patronage. But everything was to change in 1599 with the coming of the Globe. The Rose simply couldn't compete. Henslowe, faced with rising rents, struggled on for a couple more years but eventually decided to have the playhouse pulled down and shifted his interests towards bear-baiting!

In 1603 on the death of Elizabeth I and the succession of James I, Shakespeare's company, the Lord Chamberlain's Men, became the King's Men.

James by the grace of God etc. To all justices, mayors, sheriffs, constables, headboroughs and other our officers and loving subjects greeting. Know ye that We of our special grace, certain knowledge and mere motion, have licensed and authorised and by these presents do license and authorise these our servants, Lawrence Fletcher, William Shakespeare, Richard Burbage, Augustine Phillipps, John Hemming, Henry Condell, William Sly, Robert Armin, Richard Cowley and the rest of their associates freely to use and exercise the art and faculty of playing comedies, tragedies, histories, interludes, morals, pastorals, stage-plays, and such others like as they have already studied or hereafter shall use or study, as well for the recreation of our loving subjects as for our solace and pleasure when we shall think good to see them during our pleasure.

*And the said comedies, tragedies, histories,
interludes, morals, pastorals, stage-plays and
such like to shew and exercise publicly to their
best commodity, when the infection of the plague
shall decrease, as well within their now usual
house, called the Globe, within our county of
Surrey, as also within any town-halls or
moothalls or other convenient places within the
liberties and freedom of any other city, university
town or borough whatsoever within our said
realms and dominions. Willing and commending
you and every of you as you tender our pleasure
not only to permit and suffer them herein
without any your lets and hindrances or
molestations during our said pleasure, but also
to be aiding and assisting them such former
courtesies as hath been given to men of their
place and quality, and also what further favour
you shall show to these our servants, for our
sake, we shall take kindly at your hands. In
witness whereof etc. witness ourself at
Westminster the nineteenth of May.*

In 1613, during a performance of *Henry VIII* at the Globe, a piece of wadding fired from a stage cannon lodged in the thatch of the roof. It smouldered for a while and then burst into flames.

> *Upon Saint Peter's Day last, the play-house or Theater, called the Globe, upon the Bankside near London, by negligent discharging of a peal of ordinance (cannon), close to the south-side thereof, the thatch took fire, and the wind sodainly disperst the flame round about, and in a very short space the whole building was quite consumed, and no man hurt; the house being filled with people to behold the play of Henry VIII. And the next Spring it was new builded in far fairer manner than before.*
>
> *Howes continuation of Stowe's Annales*

– Notes –

– Notes –

– Notes –

Built of wood, and with a thatched roof, it didn't take long for the flames to destroy the Globe completely. Thomas Larkin sent word of the fire to Sir Thomas Pickering on June 30th, 1613...

No longer since than yesterday, while Burbage's company were acting at the Globe the play of Henry VIII, and there shooting off certain chambers in way of triumph, the fire catched and fastened upon the thatch of the house, and there burned so furiously, as it consumed the whole house, all in less than two hours, the people having enough to do to save themselves.

– Notes –

– *Notes* –

Considering how quickly the Globe burned down it was miraculous that no-one was seriously injured. Sir Henry Wotton included the following in his note to Sir Edmund Bacon on July 2nd 1613, pointing out one man's lucky escape...

Now, King Henry making a masque at the Cardinal Wolsey's house, and certain chambers being shot off at his entry, some of the paper, or other stuff, wherewith one of them was stopped, did light on the thatch, where being thought at first but an idle smoke, and their eyes more attentive to the show, it kindled inwardly, and ran round like a train, consuming within less than an hour the whole house to the very grounds. This was the fatal period of that virtuous fabric, wherein yet nothing did perish but wood and straw, and a few forsaken cloaks; only one man had his breeches set on fire, that would perhaps have broiled him, if he had not by the benefit of a provident wit put it out with bottle ale.

Is it just a coincidence that Philip Henslowe and Jacob Meade entered into a contract with Gilbert Katherens for the demolition and rebuilding of the Hope playhouse on August 29th, 1613, just two months after the fire at the Globe? Perhaps the recent destruction of the main theatrical competition provided what they saw as a chink in the wall of opportunity to grab the audiences and plays for themselves...

Following the fire, the Globe was rebuilt on its original foundations. Plays continued to be performed there until the outbreak of Civil War in 1642, when it was closed by the Puritans. The Globe was demolished two years later.

– Notes –

– Notes –

– Notes –

William Shakespeare

He was a man, take him for all in all,
I shall not look upon his like again.

Hamlet, Act I, sc ii

William Shakespeare is without doubt our best-known dramatist, and yet very little is actually known about his life. All we can say for certain is that this remarkable Elizabethan came from Stratford-upon-Avon and, although his actual date of birth remains unknown, he was baptised on April 26th 1564 and died on April 23rd 1616.

right: William Shakespeare.

William Shakespeare's father, John Shakespeare, was a prosperous man. As well as being a burgess of Stratford (a representative of the town, sent to Parliament) he is known to have manufactured gloves, and dealt in wool and any other market where he saw an opportunity to make a profit. He rose through the ranks from the posts of chamberlain and alderman to high bailiff. In 1557 he married the daughter of his father's landlord, Mary Arden. The Ardens had been prominent Warwickshire gentry since before the Norman Conquest and some of the family had held places in the royal household of Henry VII.

– *Notes* –

– Notes –

– Notes –

John and Mary Shakespeare's first children were both girls, who died in their infancy. Their third child was William, who managed to escape the plague that ravished Stratford during 1564, the year of his birth. Two further daughters, Joan and Anne and three more sons, Gilbert, Richard and Edmund, were born, all of whom survived to adulthood, except Anne who died at the age of 8 when William was 15.

In *As You Like It*, Shakespeare looks back to the days of childhood, describing perhaps from his own experience...

> *...the whining school-boy, with his satchel*
> *And shining morning face, creeping like snail*
> *Unwillingly to school.*

> *As You Like It*, Act II, sc vii

– *Notes* –

– Notes –

John Shakespeare's fortunes failed, it seems, from about 1578. In 1589 it was recorded that he had no goods worth seizing for debt. He did, however, regain some property and some esteem in the community by the 1590s. While William was making a name for himself as a dramatist, his father seems to have lived a reasonably comfortable life until his death in 1601.

– Notes –

– Notes –

In 1596 John Shakespeare, aided by the success of his son William, applied to the College of Heralds for the right to assume a family coat of arms. The grant of arms was the official sign of the status of gentleman. One of the Heralds, William Dethick, considered that granting arms to 'Shakespeare the player' would be improper, but this objection was overruled.

Stratford-upon-Avon, William Shakespeare's birthplace, is thought by many to represent the 'heart of England'. The countryside surrounding it is breathtaking, with its river, meadows, woodlands and wildflowers. At the time that Shakespeare was growing up, there were less than one and a half thousand inhabitants scattered through the community in half-timbered houses and cottages. The main buildings would have been the stately church by the river and the Guildhall which, from time to time, hosted plays. In spite of its tranquillity, the area did not escape the ravages of the plague, and disease was the frequent follower of the autumn floods.

– Notes –

– Notes –

right: seventeenth-century woodcut
of a rural scene.

Shakespeare's rural childhood could have provided him with the poetic inspiration he expresses in *As You Like It*...

> *And this our life, exempt from public haunt,*
> *Finds tongues in trees, books in the running*
>   *brooks,*
> *Sermons in stones, and good in every thing.*
> *I would not change it.*

As You Like It, Act II, sc i

– Notes –

– Notes –

On November 27th, 1582 William Shakespeare was given licence to marry a woman named Anne Whateley – this was annulled immediately due to the fact that a different Anne (the famous Hathaway) was carrying his child. So at the age of eighteen Shakespeare married Anne Hathaway, 8 years his senior. By 1585, when Shakespeare left Stratford for London, the couple had three children.

> *...men are April when they woo, December when they wed: maids are May when they are maids, but the sky changes when they are wives.*

> *As You Like It*, Act IV, sc i

– Notes –

– Notes –

right: old London Bridge, from
a seventeenth-century engraving by
Cornelius Visscher.

In 1592 Shakespeare's name appeared in a pamphlet by Robert Greene, where he was listed as an actor/player. Prior to this it is not known, with any certainty, exactly what Shakespeare's movements were in the City.

127

– Notes –

– Notes –

There is mention of Shakespeare in the accounts of the Treasurer of the Chamber suggesting that he acted twice alongside Richard Burbage (his chief tragic actor) as a member of the Lord Chamberlain's Men. These plays would have been performed for Queen Elizabeth I during Christmas 1594. It is also accepted that in 1598 Shakespeare helped stage Ben Jonson's first comedy *Every Man in his Humour*, in which he played the character of Knowell.

right: Robert Armin, one of Shakespeare's contemporaries in the Lord Chamberlain's Men.

After seeing performances of the two parts of Shakespeare's *Henry IV*, the Queen was so pleased with the character of Falstaff, the cowardly knight, that she commanded Shakespeare to feature him in one more play. She wished to see Falstaff in love, with the result that *The Merry Wives of Windsor* was written.

How ill white hairs become a fool and jester!
I have long dreamt of such a kind of man,
So surfeit-swelled, so old, and so profane;
But, being awak'd, I do despise my dream.
Make less thy body hence, and more thy grace;
Leave gormandizing; know the grave doth gape
For thee thrice wider than for other men...

Henry IV part II, Act V, sc v

– Notes –

– Notes –

– *Notes* –

In 1593, in the London district of Deptford, an event took place which was to result in William Shakespeare emerging as the foremost of London's actor-playwrights: Christopher Marlowe, a talented poet and dramatist, perhaps Shakespeare's greatest competition, was knifed to death during a tavern brawl. Marlowe, whose works include *Tamburlaine*, *The Tragedy of Dr Faustus*, *The Jew of Malta* and *Edward II*, was only 29 when he died.

The official story was that Marlowe fell into argument with 'Ingram Ffrysar, late of London, gentleman' over payment of the bill, and moved on him in anger. Ingram struggled in self-defence and stabbed Marlowe over his right eye, killing him instantly.

Other accounts of the evening's events have Marlowe, who was considered to be a spy, meeting three secret agents in the tavern. Perhaps there wasn't an argument at all... What actually happened is impossible to guess – dramatic stories and rumours surrounding Marlowe were common.

– Notes –

Ben Jonson was born in 1572, eight years after Shakespeare. He gained his royal pension by 1616; making him, in effect, Poet Laureate; he was also an honourary graduate of both Oxford and Cambridge. To some he was as popular a playwright as Shakespeare, his plays include: *Everyman in his Humour* and *Everyman out of his Humour*, *Cynthia's Revels*, *The Poetaster*, *Volpone*, *The Silent Woman*, *The Alchemist* and *Bartholomew Fair*. He was considered better at comedies than tragedies, two of which were stage failures.

Jonson was a colourful character, and was off fighting the Spanish in Flanders before his twentieth birthday. He found himself on trial for murder in 1598, having killed a man in a duel. Jonson also wrote masques for King Charles I. He died in 1637 and left us the affectionate term for Shakespeare, whom he addressed as 'Sweet Swan of Avon'.

Soul of the Age!
The applause! delight! the wonder of our stage!
My Shakespeare, rise; I will not lodge thee by
Chaucer, or Spencer, or bid Beaumont lie
A little further, to make thee a room:
Thou art a monument, without a tomb,
And art alive still, while thy book doth live,
And we have wits to read, and praise to give.

To the Memory of My Beloved,
the Author, Mr. William Shakespeare,
Ben Jonson

Working in the Elizabethan theatre was not the precarious career that one might imagine. Shakespeare's earnings as a performer and writer were such that in 1597 he was able to purchase one of the largest houses in Stratford, New Place, for £60. He also had shares in two theatres, the Globe and the Blackfriars, from which he enjoyed the profits.

– Notes –

left: the Globe, from a seventeenth-century
engraving by Cornelius Visscher.

– Notes –

– Notes –

– Notes –

S hakespeare's early work is very difficult to date
accurately, but it is widely believed that his first
completely original play was *Love's Labour's Lost*,
written around 1591. This is very much conjecture, as
the first folio of the play carried no dates.

> *When daisies pied and violets blue*
> *And lady-smocks all silver-white*
> *And cuckoo-buds of yellow hue*
> *Do paint the meadows with delight,*
> *The cuckoo then, on every tree,*
> *Mocks marred men; for thus sings he,*
> *Cuckoo:*
> *Cuckoo, cuckoo, – O, word of fear,*
> *Unpleasing to a married ear!*

Love's Labour's Lost, Act V, sc ii

Francis Meres, the eminent Master of Arts, provides one of the best insights into the chronology of Shakespeare's works. In his *Palladis Tamia, Wits Treasury* written in 1598 he gives a list of plays which is invaluable in dating them. He mentions only one that seems to be lost – *Love's Labour's Won* – unless we know it by a different name.

> As Plautus and Seneca are accounted the best
> for Comedy and Tragedy among the Latines, so
> Shakespeare among the English is the most
> excellent in both kinds for the stage: for Comedy,
> witness his Gentlemen of Verona, his Errors, his
> Love Labours Lost, his Love Labours Wonne,
> his Midsummers night dreame, and his
> Merchant of Venice; for Tragedy, his Richard the
> 2, Richard the 3, Henry the 4, King John,
> Titus Andronicus, and his Romeo and Juliet.

– Notes –

Edward Dowden was Professor of English Literature at the University of Dublin in the late nineteenth century. In *Shakspere, A Critical Study of His Mind and Art,* 1875, he outlines four specific periods of Shakespeare's creativity. First, from about 1590 to 1595–96 (IN THE WORKSHOP), years of dramatic apprenticeship and experiment: secondly, from about 1595–96 to about 1600–01 (IN THE WORLD), the period of the English Historical plays and the mirthful and joyous comedies; thirdly, from 1601 to about 1608 (OUT OF THE DEPTHS), the period of grave or bitter comedies and of the great tragedies; last, from about 1608 to 1611–13 (ON THE HEIGHTS), the period of the romantic plays, which are at once grave and glad, serene and beautiful.

– Notes –

In 1611 William Shakespeare retired to Stratford, where he died on 23rd of April 1616 on, or around, his 52nd birthday.

> *Good friend, for Jesu's sake forbear*
> *To dig the dust enclosed here.*
> *Blest be the man that spares these stones*
> *And cursed be he that moves my bones.*

Inscription on Shakespeare's tomb

– Notes –

– Notes –

– Notes –

The Elizabethan Theatre

O for a Muse of fire, that would ascend
The brightest heaven of invention,
A kingdom for a stage, princes to act,
And monarchs to behold the swelling scene!

Henry V, Prologue

– Shakespeare at the Globe –

At the end of the sixteenth century there were probably no more than a handful of public theatres in England and these were mainly concentrated in London. Mostly octagonal or circular in structure, with boxed balconies and cobbled courtyards, they took their design from the inn yards where travelling bands of players would have performed. The auditorium in an Elizabethan theatre was formed by a large round pit which was open to the sky and provided standing room for the poorer spectators. Around the walls on three levels were covered balconies with seats for wealthier patrons.

– Notes –

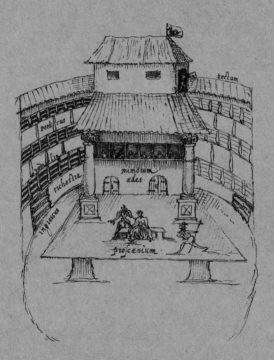

The stage in an Elizabethan theatre was large and jutted out into the pit. There was little or no scenery, so that nothing obscured the audience's view. This lack of scenery had to be compensated for by the imaginations of the audience and the skill of the actors and playwrights. This was not an easy feat considering that the audience would not have been very well travelled and many of them were certainly uneducated.

left: sketch of the interior of the Swan theatre made in about 1596 from a drawing by Johannes de Witt.

Shakespeare often used the metaphor of the play and player, and the theme of the 'play within a play' was common, as in *A Midsummer Night's Dream*, and here, in *Hamlet*:

> *Is it not monstrous that this player here,*
> *But in a fiction, in a dream of passion,*
> *Could force his soul so to his own conceit*
> *That from her working all his visage wann'd;*
> *Tears in his eyes, distraction in's aspect,*
> *A broken voice, and his whole function suiting*
> *With forms to his conceit? And all for nothing!*

> *Hamlet*, Act II, sc ii

– *Notes* –

In the Prologue to *Henry V*, Shakespeare stresses the power of the playwright's words and the importance of the audience's creative vision:

> *Think, when we talk of horses, that you see them*
> *Printing their proud hoofs i'th' receiving earth;*
> *For 'tis your thoughts that now must deck our*
> *   kings,*
> *Carry them here and there, jumping o'er times...*

– Notes –

It was the playwright's job to compensate for the lack of physical scenery in the theatre by using rich and evocative descriptions. One way of conjuring up images was through constant reference to physical aspects of the scene. In Act V, sc i, of *The Merchant of Venice*, which is set at night, every character refers to the moonlight. As most plays were performed during the afternoon, the actors' frequent comments about the time of day would have helped to reinforce it in the minds of the audience.

How sweet the moonlight sleeps upon this bank!
Here will we sit, and let the sounds of music
Creep in our ears; soft stillness and the night
Become the touches of sweet harmony.
Sit, Jessica: look, how the floor of heaven
Is thick inlaid with patines of bright gold;
There's not the smallest orb which thou behold'st
But in this motion like an angel sings
Still quiring to the young-ey'd cherubins;
Such harmony is in immortal souls,
But, whilst this muddy vesture of decay
Doth grossly close it in, we cannot hear it.

Merchant of Venice, Act V, sc i

– Notes –

Shakespeare expresses the creative power of the poet's, art in *A Midsummer Night's Dream.*

> The lunatic, the lover, and the poet,
> Are of imagination all compact.
> One sees more devils than vast hell can hold;
> That is the madman. The lover, all as frantic,
> Sees Helen's beauty in a brow of Egypt.
> The poet's eye, in a fine frenzy rolling,
> Doth glance from heaven to earth, from earth to
>   heaven;
> And as imagination bodies forth
> The forms of things unknown, the poet's pen
> Turns them to shapes, and gives to airy nothing
> A local habitation and a name.

> *A Midsummer Night's Dream,* Act V, sc i

– *Notes* –

– Notes –

Modern productions of Shakespeare's plays often get bogged down in the complexities of scene changes – probably in a futile attempt to compete with the richer medium of film. To the Elizabethans, the lack of scenery meant that they could create shorter scenes and often a large number of them.

Just as they had no scenery, Elizabethan theatres had no curtains which could be drawn to mark the end of a scene. Instead, 'scene ends' were often simply written into the text as part of the play using lines such as: 'Go, presently inquire, and so will I'. These were effective methods of clearing the stage, of getting on with the story and, what's more, they fitted in neatly with the action.

– Notes –

Ghosts and spirits, which frequently feature in Shakespeare's plays, were handled spectacularly by the inclusion of a stage trap (trap door). Also, at the back of the stage, there was a small area or recess which could be curtained off for dramatic appearances and exits.

Bernardo: 'Tis here!
Horatio: 'Tis here!
Marcellus: 'Tis gone!... [Exit Ghost.]
Bernardo: It was about to speak, when the cock
    crew....
Marcellus: It faded on the crowing of the cock.
Some say that ever 'gainst that season comes
Wherein our Saviour's birth is celebrated,
The bird of dawning singeth all night long;
And then, they say, no spirit can walk abroad;
The nights are wholesome; then no planets
    strike,
No fairy takes, nor witch hath power to charm,
So hallow'd and so gracious is the time.

                        Hamlet, Act I, sc i

– Notes –

– Notes –

Central to much Elizabethan drama was the balcony, which was found above the recess at the back of the stage. This could serve a multitude of uses including castle ramparts, an upper room and, of course, a balcony – as in Romeo and Juliet...

But soft! What light through yonder window breaks?
It is the east, and Juliet is the sun...
See, how she leans her cheek upon her hand!
O, that I were a glove upon that hand,
That I might touch that cheek!

Romeo and Juliet, Act II, sc ii

– Notes –

During Shakespeare's time it was the law that no woman could act. Female parts were instead played by young boys whose unbroken voices could sound like those of women. This is demonstrated in *A Midsummer Night's Dream*, when the character Bottom offers to play both male and female parts...

An I may hide my face, let me play Thisby too,
I'll speak in a monstrous little voice: 'Thisne,
Thisne!' 'Ah Pyramus, my lover dear! Thy
Thisby dear, and lady dear!'

A Midsummer Night's Dream, Act I, sc ii

right: costume of an Elizabethan country woman.

The fact that all the female roles were played by men goes some way to explain the frequency in Shakespeare's plays of young women disguising themselves as pageboys. This provided the audience with an added dimension to the action – as young male actors pretended to be girls pretending to be boys! In *Twelfth Night* the disguised Viola's mistress falls in love with her, believing her to be a young man, while Viola herself falls in love with her master...

> *How will this fadge? My master loves her dearly,*
> *And I, poor monster, fond as much on him;*
> *And she, mistaken, seems to dote on me.*
> *What will become of this? As I am man,*
> *My state is desperate for my master's love;*
> *As I am woman, now alas the day!*
> *What thriftless sighs shall poor Olivia breathe!*
> *O time, thou must untangle this, not I;*
> *It is too hard a knot for me t' untie.*

> *Twelfth Night*, Act II, sc ii

– Notes –

– Notes –

– Notes –

– Notes –

In 1599 Thomas Platter made the following entry in his diary, describing an all-male performance of *Julius Caesar* at the Globe:

> *After dinner on the 21st of September, at about two o'clock, I went with my companions over the water, and in the strewn roof-house saw the tragedy of the first Emperor Julius with at least fifteen characters very well acted. At the end of the comedy they danced according to their custom with extreme elegance. Two in men's clothes and two in women's gave this performance, in wonderful combination with each other.*

– Notes –

– The Elizabethan Theatre –

An account by Thomas Coryat, describing a visit to a theatre in Venice during 1611, shows how the Italians did things differently...

I was at one of their play-houses, where I saw a comedy acted. The house is very beggarly and base in comparison of our stately play-houses in England: neither can their actors compare with us for apparel, shews and music. Here I observed certain things that I never saw before. For I saw women act, a thing that I never saw before...

Shakespeare's plays, like other dramas produced at the time, would have been staged in the costume of the period. Directors who take on the plays today face the dilemma of whether or not to stage them in period costume that fits the language, or to go for other more modern or timeless styles. Elizabethan costumes cost the earth to get right, and with the added cost of elaborate scenery, staging the plays of Shakespeare can be a very expensive enterprise.

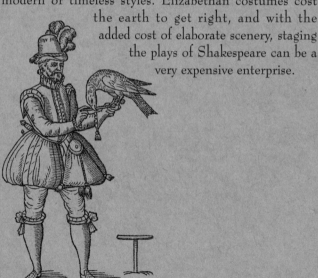

left: costume of an Elizabethan nobleman.

Once a playhouse purchased a play from an author, they were keen to protect their investment and took care not to let it fall into the hands of booksellers or publishers. Desperate to acquire copies of the most successful plays, the publishers would send along reporters to catch the words as they fell from the actors' lips and turn them into print. The results were often dire, and versions of plays appeared where the entire meaning was misinterpreted! Such an edition of Shakespeare's *Hamlet* exists with inserts from some unknown source. The same thing happened to poetry. In 1599 a volume of verse attributed to William Shakespeare was printed by a publisher called Jaggard who, it is alleged, had managed to obtain a few short pieces and added to them liberally from other sources.

– Notes –

– Notes –

– Notes –

In *Hamlet*, advice is given to players to perform naturally – and a warning is given against over-acting!

Speak the speech, I pray you, as I pronounced
it to you, trippingly on the tongue;: but if you
mouth it, as many of our players do, I had as
lief the town-crier spoke my lines. Nor do not
saw the air too much with your hand, thus...
O, it offends me to the soul to hear a robustious
periwig-pated fellow tear a passion to tatters,
to very rags, to split the ears of the groundlings,
who, for the most part, are capable of nothing
but inexplicable dumb shows and noise.

> *Hamlet*, Act III, sc ii

– Notes –

– Notes –

The audiences who flocked to the playhouses would have come from all walks of life. As John Chamberlain wrote in 1624, 'old and young, rich and poor, master and servants, papists and puritans' were among those attracted to the theatres. And there was accommodation to suit all pockets. Thomas Platter wrote, after a visit to the Globe in 1599...

Whoever cares to stand below pays only one English penny, but if he wishes to sit he enters by another door, and pays another penny, while if he desires to sit in the most comfortable seats which are cushioned, where he not only sees everything well but can also be seen, then he pays yet another English penny at another door.

– Notes –

– *Notes* –

The cheapest way to see a play was to stand in the yard; the people who did this paid only one penny and were referred to as 'groundlings'. Thomas Dekker provides a vivid description of those in this part of the audience...

Their houses smoakt every after noone with Stinkards who were so glued together in crowdes with the Steames of strong breath, that when they came foorth, their faces lookt as if they had beene per boylde.

The behaviour of an Elizabethan audience, particularly that of the groundlings, was rowdy by today's standards. They ate and drank, heckled the actors, broke into fights, threw missiles at the stage and hissed and clapped at the action.

> *These are the youths that thunder at a*
> *playhouse and fight for bitten apples.*
>
> *Henry VIII*, Act V, sc iv

– Notes –

The play-going public in Elizabethan London seem to have been a mixed and colourful group. In 1579, Stephen Gosson recorded his impressions of the crowd at a theatre in *The Schoole of Abuse.*

> *In our assemblies at plays in London, you shall*
> *see such heaving, and shoving, such itching and*
> *shouldering to sit by women, such care for their*
> *garments, that they be not trod on: such eyes to*
> *their laps, that no chips light in them: such*
> *pillows to their backs, that they take no hurt:*
> *such masking in their ears, I know not what:*
> *such giving them pippins to pass the time:*
> *such playing at foot-saunt without cards: such*
> *tickling, such toying, such smiling, such*
> *winking, and such manning them home, when*
> *the sports are ended, that it is a right comedy to*
> *mark their behaviour, to watch their conceits, as*
> *the cat for the mouse, and as good as a course*
> *of game itself, to dog them a little, or follow aloof*
> *by the print of their feet, and so discover by slot*
> *where the deer taketh soil. If this were as well*

noted as ill seen, or as openly punished as secretly practiced, I have no doubt but the cause would be seared to dry up the effect, and these pretty rabbits very cunningly ferreted from their burrows. For they that lack customers all the week, either because their haunt is unknown or the constables and officers of their parish watch them so narrowly that they dare not quetch, to celebrate the sabbath flock to theatres, and there keep a general market in bawdry. Not that any filthiness in deed is committed within the compass of that ground, as was done in Rome, but that every wanton and his paramour, every man and his mistress, every John and his Joan, every knave and his queen, are the first acquainted and cheapen the merchandise in that place, which they pay for elsewhere as they can agree.

– Notes –

– Notes –

Coming from all social spheres, the audience would have taken home with them very different appreciations of the plays they saw. The playwright was well aware of the impossibility of pleasing everyone.

> 'Tis ten to one this play can never please
> All that are here. Some come to take their ease
> And sleep an act or two; but those, we fear,
> W' have frighted with our trumpets; so, 'tis
>   clear,
> They'll say 'tis naught: others to hear the city
> Abused extremely, and to cry 'That's witty!'
> Which we have not done neither; that, I fear,
> All the expected good w' are like to hear
> For this play at this time, is only in
> The merciful construction of good women;
> For such a one we show'd 'em. If they smile,
> And say 'twill do, I know within a while
> All the best men are ours; for 'tis ill hap,
> If they hold when their ladies bid 'em clap.

King Henry VIII, Epilogue

– Notes –

The
Globe Today

When we mean to build,
We first survey the plot, then draw the model;
And when we see the figure of the house,
Then must we rate the cost...

Henry IV part II, Act I, sc iii

When the young Sam Wanamaker travelled to post-war London in 1949, he made it a priority to visit the site of Shakespeare's Globe. His disappointment was immense at finding only a bronze testimonial stuck to a brewery wall. But his imagination was fired, and he resolved to erect a memorial worthy of the greatest playwright of the Western world. His dream was to stop at nothing short of recreating the Globe, exactly as it would have been when Shakespeare was alive.

There isn't a single artefact from the period. But 'replica' hardly does justice to the care that has gone into rebuilding the Globe – felling green oaks from the Forest of Dean, Windsor Great Park and the New Forest, hand-making bricks based on Tudor models, gathering Norfolk reeds for the thatch... This in itself constitutes a form of heritage. More importantly still, by rebuilding the stage that Shakespeare wrote for, something truly remarkable is being restored.

Robert Butler, *The Independent on Sunday*, July 2nd 1995

Although there are plenty of contemporary engravings and written descriptions of the Globe, the Rose and other playhouses, the best evidence to be had for the purposes of reconstructing an Elizabethan theatre comes from the buildings themselves. In January 1989 archeologists discovered the foundations of the Rose in Southwark, north of Park Street and east of Rose Alley. Encouraged by this discovery attempts were made to locate the Globe – and nine months later, in October, a small part of its foundations were unearthed.

– Notes –

– Notes –

– Notes –

The foundations of the original Globe are buried partly under Southwark Bridge Road and partly under Anchor Terrace, a nineteenth-century listed building. Because these cannot be disturbed, further investigations of the site are being continued by non-invasive methods.

– *Notes* –

– Notes –

From the humble remains of the foundations of the Rose, archaeologists were able to gather a great many clues as to techniques and materials used by the Elizabethans in theatre building. They uncovered trenches, limestone and clunch pebble infills, a polygon of bricks which supported timbers; there was Norfolk reed rotting away that had once provided the thatch, lath and plaster, and a thick covering on the ground of a substance which later transpired to be hazelnut shells – Elizabethan popcorn? Not quite, it was an industrial by-product of soap-making and was widely used as a surface covering – providing the floor that the groundlings would have stood on. Interestingly, cherry and plum stones were found scattered among the hazelnut shells, so it seems more likely that these were the audience's snacks.

– Notes –

– Notes –

Shakespeare supplies a clue to the external structure of his theatre in the Prologue to *Henry V*, when he makes an appeal to the audience to use their powers of imagination to fill the Globe '...this wooden O...' with the armies of France and England.

> *Can this cockpit hold*
> *The vasty fields of France? Or may we cram*
> *Within this wooden O the very casques*
> *That did affright the air at Agincourt?*

– *Notes* –

Elizabethan theatres were not completely circular – wood is not a material that lends itself easily to bends and curves. Instead they were polygonal structures, with a number of straight-sided timber bays jointed together. But the question was: how many sides did it take to complete the circle? Estimates ranged from 16 to 24. Almost at the last moment, the discovery of the original Globe's foundations supplied scholars with the information they needed. Two fragments of wall revealed an angle of 162°, from which it was deduced that the Globe would have had 20 sides, and a diameter of approximately 30.5 metres (100 feet).

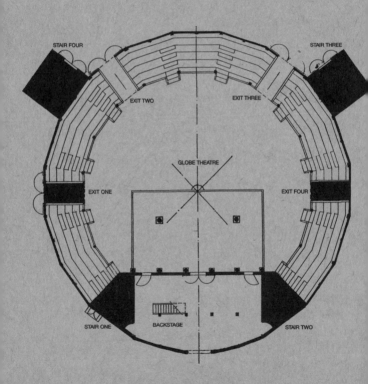

STAIR FOUR

STAIR THREE

EXIT TWO

EXIT THREE

GLOBE THEATRE

EXIT ONE

EXIT FOUR

BACKSTAGE

STAIR ONE

STAIR TWO

– *Notes* –

– Notes –

Although one of the major criteria for the rebuilding of the Globe was that it should be faithful to the original, the modern age requires a much higher standard of safety than would have been enjoyed by Elizabethan audiences. When the first Globe burned down, one witness, John Chamberlain, wrote in a letter to Sir Ralph Winwood that '...it was a great marvaile and fair grace of God, that the people had so little harm, having but two narrow doors to get out'.

The architects involved with the rebuilding of the theatre, Theo Crosby and his team at Pentagram, were determined to ensure that, for a modern audience, sitting in the Globe was not only one of the most authentic ways to experience Elizabethan theatre, but also one of the safest. Whereas the original Globe held 3,000, in order to get a licence for half that number the new Globe needed more, and wider, exits. Extra doors and stairs were incorporated, additional fire proofing materials were included deep inside the fabric of the building and an elaborate sprinkler system was installed to run the entire length of the crown of the thatch.

– Notes –

The new Globe is the first building to be constructed within the City of London with a thatched roof since 1666. This was the year of the Great Fire, when much of London was destroyed and many fine buildings were lost, including St.Pauls Cathedral, later to be redesigned by Sir Christopher Wren. Fears of a repeated disaster on this scale prompted the City authorities to place a ban on the construction of thatched buildings.

– Notes –

left: St.Pauls during the Great Fire of London, 1666.

– Notes –

– Notes –

Theo Crosby and his team went to great lengths to get every aspect of the rebuilding of the Globe right. They studied all the remaining evidence and what they couldn't discover through archeological investigations at the sites of the Globe and Rose, they looked for in other buildings of the period that had survived. The stairs at the Globe, for example, were made to resemble those found at Elizabeth I's Hunting Lodge in Chingford, Essex.

right: Hampton Court Palace, built in 1514 during the reign of Henry VIII.

One small piece of baluster discovered when excavating the Rose acted as the basis for all 315 balusters in the theatre. These are the spindles which support the wooden railing that runs around the middle galleries. Each baluster was crafted from straight grained English oak which was cut to size and then painstakingly hand turned on an authentic pole lathe.

– Notes –

Supporting the roof of the Globe's stage is a massive oak beam 13.5 metres (44 feet) in length, resting on two gigantic stage posts. This, the largest single timber in the building, had to be cut from one tree. A suitable oak, more than 21 metres (70 feet) tall, was located near Hereford. It needed a police escort on its journey to the sawmill.

right: cross section of the stage.
© Pentagram Design Limited.

First Clown: What is he that builds stronger than either the mason, the shipwright, or the carpenter?
Second Clown: The gallows-maker; for that frame outlives a thousand tenants.

Hamlet, Act V, sc i

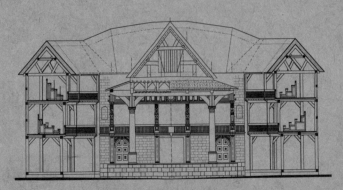

– Shakespeare at the Globe –

The Globe Theatre is now open to the public, offering the unique opportunity to experience Shakespeare's plays performed in the environment in which he intended them to be seen.

> *...it is as a <u>theatre</u> that the Globe should be judged: not as a resurrected wooden fossil, or an Elizabethan theme-park, but a place of activity and discovery...With no elaborate set designs or gimmicks to draw one's eye, one can concentrate on the words – a rare treat indeed in a town where the Bard's canon has long taken second place to unnecessary pyrotechnics and invasive concepts.*

Neil Smith, from a review of
The Two Gentlemen of Verona at the Globe
What's On, August 28th 1996

– Notes –

– Notes –

– Notes –

Although Elizabethan audiences may have been happy to watch plays in all seasons in a theatre open to the elements, the new Globe stages performances only during the summer. From about 1608, Shakespeare's company made the move to the smaller indoor playhouse at Blackfriars for the winter months. To really re-create playing conditions as Shakespeare would have known them it is necessary not only to experience the Globe, but also an indoor theatre.

– Notes –

Even less is known about the playhouse at Blackfriars than about the Globe. However, a set of plans for an indoor theatre designed by Inigo Jones came to light in Worcester College Oxford, in 1969. Although there is no evidence that these designs were ever realised during the seventeenth century, the theatre they describe, built of Tudor-style small, hand-made bricks and with a neo-classical pediment has been faithfully constructed and now stands in the Globe Centre.

right: plan of the piazza level of the Globe centre.
© Pentagram Design Limited.

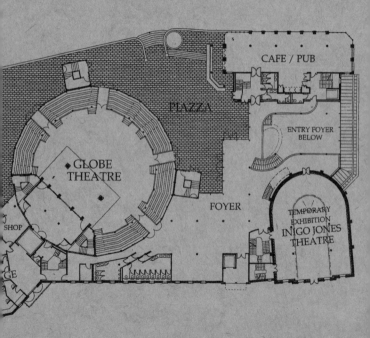

CAFE / PUB

PLAZA

ENTRY FOYER
BELOW

◆ GLOBE
THEATRE

SHOP

FOYER

TEMPORARY
EXHIBITION
INIGO JONES
THEATRE

GE

Performances of Shakespeare's plays in the new Globe and in the seventeenth-century style indoor theatre are the final realisation of Sam Wanamaker's dream, supplying a lasting and fitting memorial to one of the greatest figures in literature.

> *Our children's children*
> *Shall see this and bless heaven.*

> *Henry VIII*, Act V, sc v

– Notes –

Our revels now are ended. These our actors,
As I foretold you, were all spirits, and
Are melted into air, into thin air;
And, like the baseless fabric of this vision,
The cloud-capp'd towers, the gorgeous palaces,
The solemn temples, the great globe itself,
Yea, all which it inherit, shall dissolve
And, like this insubstantial pageant faded,
Leave not a rack behind. We are such stuff
As dreams are made on; and our little life
Is rounded with a sleep.

The Tempest, Act IV, sc i

– Notes –